divine violence

L.K. REID

Cover Design and Formatting by Moonshine Creations
Editing by Maggie Kern at Ms. K Edits

For all hollow souls searching for that one missing piece.

playlist

Dies Irae - náttúra, Vila

FALLOUT (antagonizer) - Crywolf

Goodbye - Apparat, Soap&Skin

Ritual - AWAY, Echoes

Ghostbox - AWAY, Crywolf

Tripwire - YMIR

September Rain - Cassyette

Waking Up - MJ Cole, Freya Ridings

A Drowning City - acloudskye

lost happiness - Like Saturn

Soulswap - Solitaris, holocene

Desire - Violet Orlandi

Craving - YMIR

Pixie Hollow and Purgatory - PRINCESSBRI

Villain - Missio

Down With The Sickness - Violet Orlandi, Ai Mori

author's note

I've been toying with the idea for this book for a couple of months now, and it wasn't until my own life got shaken to the core that I decided to start writing it. My grandfather hated injustice, the religious institutions that were taking something pure that people believed in only to steal, cheat and fill their own pockets without ever thinking about those that truly needed it.

He taught me to never believe blindly, even if the rest of the people I was surrounded by did. So in a way, this story is an ode to him. This entire world is an ode to him.

This book, novella, whatever you want to call it, is filled with grief, with anger, with confusion, and while our FMC is trying to do the right thing, she is also not sure what the right thing is anymore.

Society often dictates what's right and what's wrong. Our families, our friends, they do too.

This novella is a prequel to a much bigger world that's coming out next year—an introduction to these characters. I can't wait to show you more of them.

As with every one of my books, this one is a dark romance, and as such, it might not be suitable for all readers. There are mentions of suicide, a lot of grief, anger, death, violence and dub-con. It might not be the most graphic book I have ever written, but it still contains elements that could be disturbing for some people.

It is a reverse harem novella that does not contain cheating, and it ends on a cliffhanger.

And if you truly liked it, I would love to see your reviews.

"No one ever told me that grief felt so like fear."

C. S. Lewis

Twinkle twinkle little star
How I wonder what you are
Up above the world so high
How I wonder if you'll die

chapter one

ECHO

"GOOD EVENING, IGNIS. IT'S EIGHT THIRTY P.M. ,SUNDAY, October thirtieth. I'm Chelsea Donovan and this is Channel One News. It is a heartbreaking evening today in Ignis, as the news that shocked us all came just a couple of minutes ago to the studio. The body of twenty-three-year-old Clarissa Hutchins has been found today at Katoro beach by two teenagers who were passing by, trying to catch the sunset. Clarissa was reported missing last year on November first. Her parents couldn't get hold of her after she arrived at Ignis for what many presume was a party. Sources say that she attended…"

I tuned out the news anchor, my skin tingling from what I've heard already, and I focused on the dark skies hovering over Ignis. I admired the news anchor for keeping a straight face and an unwavering voice through that announcement—I wouldn't have been able to do the same.

Maybe it was because I knew grief.

It often arrived unannounced, knocking down your world like a house of cards and tearing at your flesh with a razor-sharp blade, while you choked on your misery, with your throat closing in and your eyes welling up. The wounds it left, they turned into scars that kept stinging somewhere deep inside your soul. No matter how many times you told yourself you were fine—you weren't. Not really.

Grief wasn't something tangible. I couldn't crumple it up like a piece of paper and throw it aside every time I found it hard to breathe.

It was a constant pain, a constant throbbing... A violent reminder how short life really was. And sometimes... Sometimes it quieted down, on those days when the sun shone brightly and when, for a moment, you allowed yourself a moment of peace. Where oblivion was a better option than the memories your brain kept pushing forward.

But it always came back, sometimes stronger than before. It lived in the lyrics of the songs, whispering, whispering, whispering, destroying you all over again. It existed in memories you couldn't, no, you didn't want to forget, but it would've been easier going through life without them. Some days it was a friend, others a foe, and on every October thirtieth it was a darkness clouding my mind, reminding me of everything I'd lost.

Seven years and a couple of hours, but the quiet cries of my brother still lingered on the edges of my mind, and that final, shaky breath he took as they stole away the light of my life.

The only family I had left.

The only person that truly understood me.

I've been chasing storms my entire life, hoping that someday, one of them would finally take me away from this godforsaken place. I hoped that the rain every storm brought with itself would pull me into its depths, luring me into the darkness, so that I didn't have to think about everything that was and everything that could never be. Today, more than ever, my thoughts took me back in time, to the night that tore away the innocence. To the night where demons danced their wicked little tango on the shoulders of the uncorrupted child, purring with their poisonous tongues.

Burn them.

Burn them, little one.

Burn the wicked ones.

Today, more than ever, the storm coming in lured me into its shadows, beckoning me with its thunderous voice, caressing my skin with the cold hands of wind that picked up above Ignis.

I just wished it could wash away the stain from my own heart, in the same way when it washed away the sins of that night, hiding the tracks of a wicked man and woman from the eyes of the bystanders.

Almost unconsciously, I traced the scar on my lower back, drowning out the screams and cries playing on repeat in my head

3

that often kept me awake at night. My lips pulled into a smile, my heart thundered in my chest, and deep inside, I couldn't lie to myself.

I had no regrets.

Lightning cut through the darkened sky, illuminating the violent, menacing clouds over the city, while the wind played with the strands of my hair. The taste of sorrow weeping from the group home I was placed in tainted the air, and the sound of children crying from the inside was muffled by the crash of thunder somewhere over the mountains.

Little Lorelei had struggled to adjust to the new house, despite having arrived a month ago. I almost pitied her. I knew that no matter how much she cried or how many times she called for her mom, she would never come back. But I couldn't tell that to a seven-year-old child who couldn't quite understand the meaning of death.

I thought about it, about death, more often than I should've. But how could I not, when it was the one constant thing in the first half of my life? Most of the people my age never had to deal with death. They never had to look into its eyes, realizing that it took everything away from them.

They never had to leave their home, their country, their perfect, safe world, only to be whisked from home to home, from one family to another, keeping the pieces of who they used to be, afraid that even that would be torn away from them.

They never had to hide their sins deep inside their hearts, afraid that one day all the secrets they'd been keeping would suffocate them alive.

They never had to hold the lifeless body of their sibling while the flames ate the walls of the foster home.

Marcus's last resting place.

His last cry and my rage.

Stinging pain ricocheting from my palms pulled me away from the dark thoughts of my past, and as I looked down, I could see the angry, red, moon-shaped indents appearing on my pale skin.

"You're okay," I told myself, closing my eyes momentarily. "You're going to be fucking okay," I murmured again, controlling my breathing. I could feel my chest rising and falling, my temples throbbing, but no matter how many times I've tried, this avalanche of emotions couldn't be stopped with just a few deep breaths and a promise to myself that I would be okay.

Because I wasn't okay.

I was as far from okay as one person could be, but I couldn't say that out loud.

People weren't comfortable with the reality every single tragedy brought with itself. They liked toying with the idea, talking about the tragic events of something that happened to some other people in another country, another neighborhood, another city. Yet whenever it came to their own doorstep, whenever it knocked on their perfect, white door, they crumbled, unable to deal with the events that transpired.

Even worse—they didn't know how to deal with people who went through something tragic.

I hated the pity in their eyes. I hated the unspoken words from strangers and acquaintances. I hated the "it gets better" sentence, because it didn't, really. The throbbing inside my chest might have lessened, but the anger coursing through my veins only intensified with each year that passed. I wanted to scream and shout, tear my lungs apart with the darkness suffocating my very being, but I couldn't do anything.

I was just a child. I'd learned to keep my mouth shut, to keep my head down and to walk through life as if nothing ever happened to me.

I didn't want their sad little stares, or their well-meaning words. I didn't want the whispers behind my back or the stifling attention I got back when everything happened. What could I have done with it?

Nothing.

There were no words that could soothe the gaping wound inside my chest. There were no hugs, no soft-spoken words of love and care that a child needed. There were no parents to check underneath my bed when the monsters crawled outside of my mind into the bleak reality I was living in.

There was no brother to hold my hand on the first day of school.

And now... Now I had no idea which direction my life was going to take, and it terrified me. After all the uncertainty, all the doctors, all the psychologists and changed homes, since I came to Ignis, I found something that resembled peace. Maybe it was complacency or the lack of need to change, but I'd had enough turbulence to last me for two more lifetimes. I didn't want to leave the only city I could call home.

But it wasn't like it was my choice.

Or maybe it was. But I couldn't turn my back on the only family

I had left. And that call... that fucking call that changed my life. But for better or for worse, it showed me that there was still hope. Even if it came eleven years later, it still existed.

Then why wasn't I elated?

Why wasn't I happy that in two days› time I would be leaving this city, this continent, to go back to my home country, to my home city—Corwynth?

When I'd heard that last name—my original last name—why didn't I scream from happiness? My paternal grandmother found me after years of searching for me, yet the only emotion flooding my body wasn't happiness, but sadness. It meant I would be leaving the one steady thing I had in my life.

Hearing her name, her voice as she trembled on the other side of the line, brought back the memories I have long since forgotten. My earliest memories were filled with Grandma Aurelia—her brilliant smile, her kind eyes, and a soft touch—but she was a stranger now. And I wasn't little Echo Selene Selke, ready to conquer the world with her family by her side.

I was Echo Winslow now—a sinner, just another damned soul who wished to disappear.

How was I supposed to go there, fly across the ocean, when my hollow heart lay heavily inside my chest, without the brightness that once surrounded me and without a family that used to love me?

Would she see the void swallowing my soul?

Would she see the emptiness reflecting in my eyes?

Would she love me even though my hands had blood on them,

and my mind stopped believing in dreams?

Were we the sum of our sins? Or were we the children adrift in the great, vast world, floating in the ocean of lost dreams? This funeral for souls was the only real thing I knew, so how was I supposed to move on? Was I supposed to forget or at least try to?

Happiness was as much of a stranger as my dear grandmother, living all the way across the ocean, yet I yearned for it. I needed it, but I didn't know how to ask for it.

This fortress of sorrow I'd built around my heart was the only place that felt like home.

It was easier hiding behind the empty heart, convincing yourself that you didn't deserve happiness, because those you loved never lived long enough to find theirs. Sometimes it felt as if my happiness would forever be tied to a small grave on the other side of the city. The grave that shouldn't have been the final place for my brother's pure soul.

It should've been mine.

chapter two

ECHO

I WAS AFRAID OF HEIGHTS FOR AS LONG AS I COULD remember, but sitting here on the edge of the rooftop of one of the tallest buildings in Ignis felt different. Detached from the world, looking at the strangers down on the street as they ran from one side of the sidewalk to the other, trying to evade the pouring rain, I felt invisible.

Nothing and no one could touch me up here.

I was close to heaven here. I was close to those I'd lost and far away from reality. I liked to pretend to run away from everything I was, faking a different life in my head. It was a beautiful fantasy, it was all mine.

I found this place months ago, during one of those restless nights, when every single corner of the city suffocated me and when nothing I did quieted the demons inside my head. I found this building in the middle of the darkness when my soul cried for freedom and my heart felt as if it was going to jump out of my chest.

I wasn't sure if it was sheer luck or the wicked hand of destiny, but the back entrance was unlocked, with no guards in sight. It was the first time that I'd felt alive.

The first night that the adrenaline coursed through my veins and the anger I felt was nowhere to be seen.

I rushed to the service elevator, going all the way to the last floor. I had no idea what the purpose of my quest would be, but when I saw the rooftop and the lights of the city flickering in the distance, I could finally breathe again.

Then there was him. The stranger who came every single time, no matter what hour of the night I found myself here. There was something uncanny about the way he just stood there, watching, observing, following my every move with his eyes.

He hid himself in the darkness of the night. That first time, I thought he was a guard, coming here to kick me out of the building.

But he never said a word. He never moved from his spot next to the door leading to this rooftop. Somehow, I didn't feel alone.

I bared myself to him through every move I made with my body, dancing under the stars to the sorrowful tunes of the music I brought with me. Each time, I expected him to come to me.

Each time, my yearning for this enigma of a man increased, my soul called out to him, but he always disappeared before the last beat of the song would end. Each time, I was left hollow, with a gaping hole inside my chest, waiting to be filled.

Tonight he would come—I knew he would. In the witching hour, under the guise of the night, he would come. The shadow, a man. I couldn't explain this connection I had to the faceless stranger who only ever came when my mind was crumbling.

I pulled my legs up, folding them to the side of my body, and pushed myself away from the edge of the building. My hair fell on my face, wet from the downpour, and my clothes stuck to my body, but I wanted to feel alive.

I wanted to feel something else tonight.

If this was my last night here on this rooftop, I wanted to remember it forever.

I walked back toward the center of the rooftop, stepping into the shadows. I shook off the thin jacket I had on me, leaving only the black T-shirt that was now completely molded to my body. My phone was going to be destroyed in this rain, but I couldn't find it in myself to care.

The light from the screen illuminated my face, and as I pressed play, I lowered it down to the floor, not too far from me, and covered it with my jacket, if only to provide a small protection from the rain. The downpour ended half an hour ago, and the storm that felt as if it would sweep us all away turned into a drizzling rain, only enough to remind us that it was still there.

The hushed beats from the song echoed around me—not loud enough to alert anyone of my presence here, but loud enough for me to hear it.

"Dies Irae" by náttúra reverberated around me, awakening my body, calling for my soul. Through the hushed tones, I could feel the ecstasy slowly creeping up my legs, sneaking into my bloodstream.

My body had a mind of its own, moving with the beat. There was no need to count the steps. No need to think of the choreography because this was what I did best—I improvised.

A buzz of excitement shot through me as my feet carried me from left to right, my entire being doing what it was born to do. It danced.

Dance and music were the two things I never lost. Even after everything that happened, they persisted, two faithful companions letting me vent through them.

Pulling my feet together, the first ballet position came naturally to me. Years and years of classical ballet and I could do it now, even in my sleep. My training might have stopped and the ballet I'd learned might have turned into contemporary dance rather than classical ballet, but my body still remembered every single step.

A movement to my right pulled my attention from the song and I saw him, standing there, hugged by the shadows I loved so much. I often wondered if maybe I'd imagined him. Maybe my mind started cracking under the pressure of reality, but each time I saw him, all those doubts faded away, leaving me with a renewed yearning for him.

The tribal drums with the sounds of the oriental music moved me. Slowly, fluidly, I moved in his direction, taking two steps forward, while my arms lifted above my head, floating like the wings of a bird, caressing my body in their wake.

Piercing my heart, the music floated through my body, awakening every nerve ending, every sleeping cell, until the walls I kept erected around me crumbled, leaving me bared to this man. I showed him the pain as my chest pulled inward, bending my back, while my arms hugged my body.

The arabesque to my left released the anger, as if I could kick it to the side, letting it float away from me. My breathing intensified with each new step I took, but I was alive.

I was powerful, floating over the concrete floor on this rooftop, giving it my everything.

Dancing wasn't about technique. It wasn't about counting your steps or knowing where you landed. The beauty of dance, any dance, was that you could feel everything. You could allow yourself to become something else, someone else...

There were no restraints, there were no restrictions on what you could and couldn't do. As my body bent and folded, only to be spread open again, I pushed out the darkness clouding my mind. The haunting voice coming over the speaker of my phone gave me the boost I needed.

I could see him from the corner of my eye as I performed the dance of the damned in this hymn for the dead. I could feel his eyes on my body, on my face, following my every movement.

There was something dangerous, something wild, in the air every time he was around, and I wanted to dance in his madness.

I wanted to wrap myself around his soul, around his heart, and somewhere there, hidden inside the dark chest of wonders he kept only for himself, I could finally find home.

As I leaped through the air, doing the ciseaux, my legs split and my arms outstretched, I closed my eyes, transporting myself into the fantasy of my own making. I was loved there, in that other world. I had a home. I had a purpose. I had no secrets eating me alive.

But fantasies were nothing more than dreams that could've never been, and just like the song, my fantasy had to end.

The melody I was lost in mere moments ago stopped, leaving me with the sound of rain and an ambulance rushing somewhere not too far from here. My eyes sought him, my heart thundering, foolishly thinking he would stay, that tonight would be the night.

But when I looked at the spot he'd occupied during my dance, the disappointment washed over me, killing what little hope I had.

He was gone.

Being soaked during the harsh October weather was not my idea of fun, but it didn't seem like such a bad idea hours ago. Now, as I trekked up the hill, pulling my bicycle with me, I realized that my night only went from bad to worse.

I stayed on top of that goddamn building for another hour, hoping he would come back. Hoping that I would get to live this fantasy I had in my head, but I didn't need to be a genius to know that the only companion I would have tonight would be the cold wind and the shouts of drunk frat boys roaming down the street.

So I left.

I had no idea what I was angry at. Him? Myself?

It always came back to being angry at myself if I was being completely honest. What person of sound mind would even imagine getting lost in a stranger's arms when there were so many dangers lurking from every corner of our world?

Me, that's who.

But I guess that when you had nothing else to lose, recklessness became the companion you shouldn't have craved, but it attached itself to you all the same. And me? I didn't care about the consequences.

That man, that shadow lurking in the darkness, could've been a serial killer, and I was just another silly eighteen-year-old craving attention in the forbidden places, because I had no one to tell me that I shouldn't. I shouldn't have gone there.

I should've run the first time I saw him, but the fire burning in my veins pulled me closer to him. Every time I saw him standing there, observing, I felt like the only girl in the world. Wasn't it fucked up that I needed that attention just to feel alive? Wasn't it fucked up that I couldn't go out with someone my age? I had no doubt in my mind that the faceless man was older than me.

The only people awake and out and about during the witching hour were those with souls colored in crimson, depraved enough to seek what they wanted, consequences be damned.

But no more.

I would never go back there again. I would never crave his touch. I'd be damned if I ever even thought about him.

God. What a fool I was.

Thunder rumbled in the distance, mirroring the torrent of misery and shame in my heart. The worst part of this anger inside my body was that it stemmed not from actual rage, but from the mortification of an eighteen-year-old who thought she could attract someone, while being hugged with the hands of youth and sadness.

Who would've wanted to introduce themselves to an obvious young girl pretending to be older than she was?

Sometimes I felt like I was mature beyond my age, but other times, like tonight, I could see myself for what I really was—a young fool.

A young fool looking for paradise in the dark night where only sinners and villains lived. A young fool, hopeful that someone, someday, would take me away from this madness swarming inside my head.

It didn't matter that in two days I would have everything I ever wanted, at least materialistically. I'd been dreaming for years of the moment when someone would come and say that all I went through was a dream and that I would finally get to go home.

But what was home? Was it four walls and a roof, or was it two eyes and a heartbeat? Was my home still in Corwynth or was it somewhere else in this big, beautiful world we occupied?

It still bothered me that the excitement I expected to have evaded me. Even though I wanted to be happy, I wanted to be elated, I still couldn't bring myself to it. My grandma was just on the other side of the ocean, east from here, east from my heart, waiting for me to walk inside her house.

That tremble in her voice when she called me was proof enough how relieved she was that they finally found me, and how heartbroken she was that my brother wasn't with me.

Goddammit, I wanted to feel that happiness, that tiny sparkle inside my chest, spreading light and joy through my body, but it still slept. It still hid from me, and I had no idea why. Was it because of the stranger? Was it because my soul wept for tragedy more than fortune and comedy? Was it because I yearned for toxicity more than normalcy?

Maybe if I had a time machine, I would've gone back in time, stopped my parents from ever getting out of that hotel, just so that I could have a joyful life. So much time spent on what-ifs, so many years spent with the tear-stained face, and now standing here in front of the group home I've lived in for the past couple of years, I wondered if I blew it all out of proportion. Perhaps I did?

There were traces of depravity in me, and that had nothing to do with the tragedy that struck our family. The depravity came alive from the choices I'd made, from every little mistake I'd committed. The death of my parents and my brother was maybe a catalyst for who I was today, but the rest... the rest was my own doing.

But could I change it? Could I change my DNA to accommodate the new life I wanted to have?

Dogs barked from their own little prisons and I couldn't help but feel for them. I knew what it felt like. You were free, yet confined to one singular space. You were fed, but starved for something more than food.

You were loved, but you wanted more and more and more. When would more stop being necessary? Would there ever be a day where I didn't feel as if the void was trying to swallow me whole, leaving just a broken shell of a girl that could've had everything?

I was certain that there were thousands of people thinking just like me, lost in the most crucial moments when their destiny was at stake. I just wished that there was someone to tell me what to do. To tell me how to feel. To hold my hand and tell me that everything would be alright, even if that was the biggest lie of them all.

Was it possible that the only time my heart thundered in my chest was when the danger I craved so much presented itself in front of my eyes?

I knew who owned that building. I knew what kind of depravity hid behind its closed doors. Even though I was oblivious that first time, the second, the third, fourth—I couldn't even count how many more—I knew which monster of this city owned it.

And I still went there, hoping to meet my kind of monster.

I hoped that there would be a monster out there sick enough to love a broken little girl, because that's all I ever wanted—love. For someone who claimed how cold, detached, and uncaring she was, I felt everything. I craved that closeness with another person, no matter how fucked up that same person was.

It made me sick to my stomach that I needed it to feel alive. It disgusted me that I couldn't love myself hard enough to fill in that emptiness inside my stomach.

You can't replace what you've lost with a new, shiny thing, but toxicity worked wonders. If it wasn't another lover, it was alcohol, the drugs, the need to both feel and stop feeling altogether that filled the emptiness for at least a moment, until reality came crashing with the violence.

I pressed my bike against the stone wall that surrounded our group home, and walked slowly through the main gate, almost on my tiptoes, afraid that one of the guardians would see me. Not that they cared about what I did now that I would be leaving, but they still had a reputation to uphold. If someone saw me sneaking in and out in the middle of the night, it wouldn't bode well for the other older children that still did the same.

I avoided the windows, bending down as I shuffled toward the metal stairs that were now completely covered in ivy, breathing slowly as if the sound of my breathing would alert them of my whereabouts.

My hand gripped the first rail and I pulled myself up, wincing at the squeaking sound my shoes produced. I should've worn something else other than these converse shoes, but I didn't exactly have a lot of options. Most of my things were already shipped off to Corwynth. My muscles groaned, protesting, as I pulled myself up and up and up, until I reached the window of my room.

I shouldn't have exerted myself this much while dancing, but it was too late for regrets now.

Grunting as I went over the part of the roof that extended from my window, I finally reached the small balcony I used to sit on. With the careful maneuvers, I dropped my legs down to the solid ground, thankful that I hadn't slipped tonight.

But then I saw it—my door ajar and a cigarette butt on my balcony.

I smoked, but I was careful to never leave evidence behind. Adult or not, our guardians still cared about our well-being and smoking was a very big no. I was sure I'd closed the door of the balcony.

Carefully, with my heart in my throat, I walked forward, ignoring the thundering fear gripping my shoulders, and pushed the door open wide.

"Hello?" I whispered, praying to everything that was holy that an answer wouldn't come. Did one of the other kids get into my room somehow?

I toed off my shoes and stepped inside, reveling in the warmth of the room. My eyes flickered from the door of my room to the old television standing in the corner, and all the way to the wardrobe, but nothing was out of place.

I walked toward the opposite door and turned on the light, letting it illuminate the entire room. That's when I saw it. That's when the momentary relief I felt completely disappeared, leaving me with the gripping fear once again.

There on my pillow, a stark contrast to the white sheets, a lone black rose lay, right on top of a black square box with a piece of paper on it. I approached slowly, as if what was there on my bed could jump up and bite me.

Leaning down, I could see that it wasn't just some random piece of paper. It was a music sheet, the first page of Mozart's "Requiem in D minor", the introduction to the masterpiece that some say killed him. It was there, on my bed, in my room, and I had no idea who'd placed it there.

My hand wrapped around the stem of the rose, immediately regretting it.

"Fuck," I cursed, letting it drop on the bed with a single droplet of my blood staining the white sheets. The stem was full of thorns. As I leaned down to get a better look at it, it wasn't exactly black. No, the redness peaked through the darkness, the color of blood and a crimson promise right there on my bed.

Maybe it was the shock or maybe the knowledge that someone came into my room while I wasn't here, but as I pulled the box closer to me, I could feel how heavy it was. Opening the lid, I half expected it to have scorpions or snakes inside, but what greeted me was neither.

An envelope the same color as the box was inside, resting on what seemed to be black fabric. There was no return address on the envelope, nothing but my name written in cursive in golden ink.

Echo Selene Winslow.

I dropped onto the bed, finally realizing that whoever this was, knew my middle name. The name that I haven't used in years.

My hands trembled as I opened it, careful not to tear it apart. I never expected to see an invitation inside. Maybe this was all a sick joke, but the way my heart thundered and my hands shook told me otherwise.

"Dear Ms. Winslow," I read out loud. *"You are cordially invited to Quell Island for an annual Samhain celebration by Mr. Adair."* Holy shit. *"Please make sure to bring this invitation with you, as it will serve as an entry ticket."*

I couldn't breathe. Holy motherfucking shit.

How did this get here? The Adair family was the most powerful family in the city right now, and the heir, Kairos Adair, was an enigma to all who lived here.

He rarely ever stepped into the limelight, so much so, that the local newspapers named him a beast, mentioning that he must look like one if he was never to be seen by another person. I'd also heard the rumors that the Adair family got themselves involved in the Underground World a long time ago, but those were just rumors. Right?

My eyes kept flickering over the words written with golden ink. When I turned my head to the side to look into the box, I realized that it wasn't just some random fabric sitting inside.

I pulled it out, only to see that it was a midnight black dress with long, black tulle, with crimson peeking from beneath. My hand trembled as I ran it over the corset, over the black flowers that decorated it with equally dark leaves. It was both revealing and modest with the way the corset was cut in a deep V through the middle, leaving little to the imagination.

Two thin straps connected the corset with the back, decorated with black vines. As I turned the dress, I could see that the back was completely open.

The light in the room flickered as thunder struck somewhere in the distance. My breathing turned shallow as my eyes zeroed in on the last piece inside the box. A golden mask sat there, decorated with intricate swirls and patterns, glinting underneath the soft glow of the light.

I ran my fingers over the cold surface of the mask, utterly speechless, but at the same time—excited.

It wasn't until I saw the final note just underneath the mask that my excitement started mixing with dread and fear.

The Maiden and the wolves. Are you ready to play the game, little sparrow?

What in the fuck?

chapter three

ECHO

MY GRANDFATHER ONCE TOLD ME ONLY PEOPLE
WITH no sins and nO regrets walked with their heads held high,
because no one could ever tell them that they didn't deserve
everything they had.

What would he think of me now as I walked down the docks
with my head lowered down, covered with the hood of my jacket,
while the sins of yesterday and all the secrets I'd held close to my
heart fought for dominance somewhere deep inside? Would he be
proud of who I'd become? Would any of them be?

The cold metal of a Swiss pocketknife pressed against my thigh, strapped with the old belt I pulled out from my wardrobe. I should've torn that invitation up as soon as I'd read it, but something wicked, something dark, whispered, pulled and taunted, and I couldn't bring myself to do it.

I shouldn't be here, walking toward the large group of people gathered in front of the massive, black boat that would take us all the way to Quell Island. Rich and entitled people had that air around them that made you know, even without knowing who exactly they were. That you were in the presence of someone that considered themselves to be better than you.

As I closed the distance between us, I could see the wide-eyed stares on those that held their masks in their hands, no doubt wondering, much like me, what the fuck was I doing here.

Females gathered in small groups leered at me, while men openly ogled me. My gut churned, threatening to spill the few miserable pieces of bread I'd managed to eat today. I wanted to make myself invisible, smaller somehow, tucked into the dark corner as an observer of these people. They both fascinated and angered me with their judging eyes and the whispers rolling off their tongues, but I reveled in the knowledge that they had no idea who I was.

I recognized some of them.

Tycoons, royalties in their own way, men and women powerful enough to have a say about things in today's society, yet most of them kept their mouths shut. They hid behind the iron gates of their perfect homes, uncaring for the ones living on the other side of their picture-perfect lives.

Because on the other side, where the rest of us lived, perfection was only a faraway dream.

I might not have known the struggles of group homes when I was a child, but I knew now. I could see Vera and the other guardians at home, struggling to make ends meet.

Government funding was not enough for the amount of abandoned children who needed a safe place to live in. We needed food, clothes, money, to at least survive, yet these people that could help, that could ease the suffering of millions without even making a dent in their own pockets, simply turned their heads to the other side. It was easier pretending that nothing ever touched you, rather than helping those in need.

I despised them.

Their beauty was only skin deep, stained with their selfishness and cruel acts. I was an outsider here, a lost lamb within a pack of wolves that all knew each other in one way or another. Yet for all my wrongdoings, I could still sleep at night, knowing that I did everything I could to cleanse this earth from people like them.

I was sure that they couldn't say the same.

I passed next to a stunning blonde whose smiling face graced the billboard above the Downtown Cinema. She looked ethereal on that billboard, as if she came from some other universe, giving us mere mortals a taste of perfection just by looking at her.

Anastasia Dawson, if that was even her real name.

But as her eyes connected with mine and those lips pulled into an ugly sneer, I knew that the only other universe she could've walked in from was hell and there was no hiding it.

She didn't need to know my name or where I came from to know that I didn't belong in their circles, and frankly, I didn't even want to try to fit in. If it wasn't for the sheer curiosity that would've eaten me alive had I not come here, I wouldn't be here.

People from my world didn't mix with them and I now dreaded the rest of the night, seeing that I was the only one that didn't belong here. I was wearing the nicest dress, but it was hidden by this ugly jacket I found in my wardrobe. I was wearing the golden mask that came in the package, but I was still me.

Clothes couldn't hide what lay deep beneath our skin, and these people... They were the vultures I would've otherwise avoided for the rest of my life.

My anxiety spiked with each new step I took, walking between them, trying to find a place I could stand, while my hands clutched at the front part of my dress, holding onto the lace like a lifeline. The invitation was safely tucked in the inside pocket of my jacket, as was my phone. I knew I was about to step into the lion's den.

I just couldn't help but wonder—why me?

I knew none of these people. I had no connections to the Adair family except for my little escapades in that building. Could it have been—

"You look a little bit lost." A deep timbre of a voice stopped me in my tracks just as I was about to come closer to the boat.

Letting go of my dress, I let the length of it cover the black boots I wore instead of some fancy heels and tucked my hands inside the pockets of my jacket. My eyes traveled up, over the expensive-looking suit that must have been tailored to the man standing in front of me, over the square, wide shoulders taking so much space, all the way to the sharp jawline covered in the five-o'clock shadow of a beard, to the most striking pair of blue eyes I had ever seen.

His face, much like mine, was covered with a mask. But where mine was golden with intricate swirls, making it look more feminine, his was black. Crimson streaks covered it, as if they were imitating blood vessels just thrown together.

There was nothing soft in this man.

His full lips were set in a grim line, and even under this dim light, I could see how smooth his olive skin was. His dark hair, almost the same color as mine, looked as if someone had continuously run their fingers through it.

He oozed power, confidence, and even though his words didn't hold an accusation in them, I felt so small underneath his gaze that I wanted to turn and run far away from this place.

There was something violent hidden in those blue depths. Something depraved that made my breath hitch and my heartbeat fasten. Something that beckoned me, called to me. If I didn't know better, I would've said that it was the same kind of energy that called to me from the stranger on that rooftop.

Could he be… No. Absolutely no.

What would be the chances?

I knew I stared at him like a deer caught in the headlights, but the words were stuck in my throat. No matter how many times I swallowed, they just wouldn't roll off my tongue. His lips moved gracefully, but the ringing in my ears made it impossible to hear him.

"Are you?" he asked, leaning down closer to me. The scent of rain, cigarettes, and oak wood wafted through my nose. Heady with the sudden onslaught of yearning, of need, to touch him, to wrap my hands around his body, almost knocked me off my feet.

But I steadied myself.

"I'm sorry, what?" I finally spoke, hating how small and insignificant my voice sounded.

I stepped back as he chuckled, surprising me momentarily. His facial expression changed, going from stern to relaxed in a matter of seconds.

"I said…" he leaned even closer, coming all the way to my ear. I could feel his breath caressing the sensitive skin of my earlobe, and even though his hands never came in contact with any part of my body, I could feel every word deep inside my soul. "You look a little bit lost, Sparrow."

"Sparrow?" I turned to look at him, almost bumping his nose with mine. Flustered, I stepped back, putting some distance between the two of us. "I am most definitely not lost," I replied before he could say another word. "Are you? Lost, I mean?"

"No." He shook his head and crossed his hands one over the other, right in front of his body. "I am exactly where I'm supposed to be."

There it was. That glint, as if he knew something I didn't, a secret swirling behind those cerulean eyes.

"Well." I cleared my throat and mirrored his position as I removed my hands from my pockets. "I believe I am where I'm supposed to be as well."

He tilted his head to the side, his eyes never leaving mine. "That you are."

Unlike the other men with leering stares and hunger in their eyes as they saw me pass by, this one was completely different. The condescending looks I kept receiving from all the men and women evaporated from my memory into thin air, replaced by the stare of this stranger who rendered me speechless in the matter of seconds.

"I think that the rest might not agree with you and me." I smiled and looked over my shoulder at the crowd behind us who were trying not to look our way, yet failing. "But I don't really care," I told him proudly.

"And you shouldn't."

We stood there, staring at each other as if the rest of the world didn't exist. Even though I didn't know his name nor did he know mine, I had never felt more seen. My initial thought was that he would be another condescending prick, asking me what I was doing here when it was clear that I didn't belong in their social circles.

But he wasn't.

"My name is Echo," I said first when it was obvious that he wouldn't say another word. I extended my hand toward him, ready for a handshake. I never expected him to take my hand and pull it all the way to his lips, kissing the top part as if we were lords and ladies in some other time.

The moment his lips connected with my cold skin, I shivered, letting it run through me as his eyes connected with mine.

"Echo." He murmured my name as if he was trying the taste of it on his lips, and slowly moved back from me, letting my hand drop.

I felt cold and dizzy without him holding me, and I loved and hated that this man had such a strong influence on me.

"My name is Alexander." He grinned. "Alexander Hale."

I paled.

Hale came from the Eastern World, just like my family did. They were practically royalty back in my home country, having ties with the actual royal family now. And I didn't mean the distant cousins who had just a smidge of royal blood in their veins.

The head of the family was second in line for the crown itself. If that didn't make me step away, I had no idea what would.

His oldest son, Alexander, was the CEO of Hale Industries, having his fingers in the retail fashion industry as well as lodging. This man standing in front of me wasn't just out of my league—he was from a different universe.

"Well, Mr. Hale—"

"Mr. Hale is my father, Echo. Well, royal pain in the ass as well, but I am just Alex." His eyes twinkled as if he found it amusing how flustered and lost for words I was.

"Okay," I mumbled. "Just Alex. It was nice meeting you."

"Come on now, Sparrow. I would like to think that it was more than nice."

Was it? Or did I imagine the way his eyes couldn't leave mine and the way his body, as if having a mind of its own, started coming closer to me as if he too couldn't bear to stand too far away?

"Why do you call me sparrow?" I blurted out, curious beyond measure. No one had ever given me a nickname. No one had ever had a chance to do so. Having it come from him made it so much more interesting.

"People often overlook them, searching for swans, hummingbirds, and doves, but sparrows... they are stronger than all those pretty little birds that are trying too hard to be noticed. Sparrows would much rather go unseen, small but resilient. Even though they might seem fragile, I believe that there's fire in those little bodies waiting to be released."

Once again, I was rendered speechless.

Maybe I should've been angry that he'd compared me to a plain looking bird but hearing why and his reasoning made me look at it in a completely new light.

"Well." I gulped down the nerves that were threatening to surface. "No one has ever described me in such a manner. I kinda like it."

"I like it, too," he said, but there was a deeper meaning behind those plain words.

I wanted to stay here and chat with him the entire night, but things like that weren't reserved for me. I could already feel the daggers being sent my way from the crowd behind us. The last thing I wanted was to have some other girl destroying my night just because I dared to speak with the man that half of them wanted to have.

I wanted to see what this party was about. It was a public secret. I always wondered what it would be like feeling like a princess for at least one night.

And now I had my chance.

I gathered my dress again. I didn't miss the twinkle in his eye when he saw my plain black boots beneath the beautiful lace tickling my legs, but he kept his mouth shut and so did I.

"It was truly nice meeting you, Alex." I smiled at him as I took two steps closer, trying to pass next to him. "I hope you have an amazing night," I said, just as I was about to walk away.

But he stopped me.

His warm hand wrapped around my bicep, halting me in my steps.

A very un-ladylike squeak erupted from me when he pulled me closer to his body. The side of my breast brushed against his hard front and as I looked up at him, I gasped at the fire brewing in his eyes.

"Why are you running away?" he whispered. "Did I say something wrong?"

"N-No," I stammered. "But I didn't want to bother you."

"Did I say you were bothering me?" He narrowed his eyes at me as I shook my head. "Then don't assume something. Trust me, darling," he let go of my arm and instead wrapped his arm around my shoulders, "if I don't want to talk to somebody, I simply ignore them. You, on the other hand," he looked down at me as we walked toward the boat, "you fascinate me."

"I fascinate you only because I am not like the rest of them," I bravely said, regretting my words as soon as they left my mouth. "Shit." I stopped and moved away from his embrace. "I'm sorry. I didn't mean it in—"

"Yeah, you did." He laughed. "And that's absolutely fine. Let me tell you a secret…"

He lowered his head down as if he really was going to tell me something special.

"I hate half of these people and the other half I don't even know. It's always the same crowd, the same stories, and the same, constant whining about their designer shit as if I give a fuck. I'm glad you're not like them. You're real."

You're real, echoed inside my head.

Was I really? I might not be living in an ivory tower, detached from the rest of the world, but there were days where I didn't really know who I was anymore. Constantly stuck in the limbo between being a sinner or a saint, I had no idea which part of me was real anymore.

But if he thought I was real, I could pretend for one night. I could tell him everything he wanted to hear and some more, but I couldn't give him more than that.

He didn't get to see the real me.

"You are not what I expected," I said. "Not that I knew you would be here tonight, but still."

"What did you expect me to be?" he asked as we continued walking toward the boat.

"A pompous prick?" I squinted at him. "An entitled, spoiled rich man who couldn't see further than his own nose?"

"Ouch." He placed a hand over his heart, feigning hurt. "You wound me, little one. Not all of us are that bad, you know?"

I shrugged. "I am yet to be proven wrong, Alex. But I guess that you're on the right track. As long as you don't leave me with them."

And by them, I meant all the females who would most likely like to throw me into the water for merely walking with him.

"Don't worry," he whispered just as a honking sound came from the boat. "You'll be safe with me." He pulled me with him over the metal board erected for us to step onto the boat, all the while holding my hand in his, as if I would slip away if he didn't hold on to me. "I think you're going to love it tonight."

"I hope so too," I added. "It is my last night in Ignis."

Something flashed in his eyes as he looked down at me, but it disappeared and that carefree look came back again before I could question it.

"Well then," he mumbled as we stepped onto the boat. "Let's make sure it is an unforgettable one."

chapter four

ECHO

QUELL ISLAND WAS JUST A WAYWARD THOUGHT THE whole time I lived in Ignis, yet I, just like many others, heard the stories about the tragic history of this beautiful place.

The island existed for as long as people could remember. A natural habitat for several species of birds and lizards, but it wasn't its flora and fauna that made it so interesting that even the tourists that came to Ignis wanted to see it, even if it was only from afar.

Back in the sixteen hundreds, a wealthy couple moved from the Eastern World to the Western World, wanting to start a new life. And even though they held the picture of a perfect family, there were sinister things lurking behind closed doors. Only Mr. And Mrs. Hatherow with their children knew the truth.

The island that was once bare now held the secrets of that family and all the monstrosities they had committed. The eldest son of the couple, Jacob Hatherow, was every woman's dream at that time, but none of them knew the wickedness hiding behind his kind smile.

In the time where White people thought they were better than other races just because of their fair skin color, blue eyes and blond hair, depraved secrets hid behind the walls of the mansions of those wealthy families.

Jacob Hatherow was a monster who tortured the women that worked for them. Women that weren't fair. Women that didn't have a family to support them and help them.

The story said that he lured them into his web of lies with sweet words and promises of tomorrow, only to torture them in the basement of the house, before having sexual intercourse with them. More than fifty bodies were found buried on the other side of the island, but Jacob Hatherow never paid for his crimes. I wished he was the only monster that used to exist on this side of the continent.

His sister was even worse.

I shivered at the mere thought of everything she did to both men and women who were foolish enough to trust her. Wrapping my arms around my middle, I stared at the dark water and the flickering lights peeking through the tree line of the island.

Some said that to this day, you could hear the screams of all those poor souls who lost their lives to the wicked brother and sister. Others warned to stay away from the maze that occupied the middle area of the island, just behind the grand mansion the Adair family refurbished when they moved in.

I had no idea what to believe, but I knew very well that every single story held at least a little bit of truth. What happened here wasn't just some cautionary tale older people told just to scare little children.

Monsters were real.

They were real back then and they were real now. The only difference was that now they knew how to hide their true faces better.

An unfamiliar voice murmured behind me, "Feeling cold?"

Startled, I turned around, halfway expecting to see Alex there. He'd gone inside to talk to the captain, but he wasn't the one standing not too far away from me.

Murmurs came through the open door of the boat from the crowd talking inside, but the crowd wasn't what had me standing up from the bench I was sitting on.

Where Alex was dark, broad, and much taller than me—all-around reminding me of an Aegean hero from the stories of a long time ago—this one looked like a fallen angel.

They were a stark contrast really, and I had no idea if it was the wealth and status in the world that made these men look like GQ models, or something in their water. I couldn't take my eyes off him.

"Would you like to have my jacket?" he asked and came closer to where I stood. He didn't take up too much space, but I could feel him everywhere around me.

His blond hair was shorter on the sides and longer on the top, artfully arranged no doubt by a personal stylist. His tuxedo fit him like a second skin, leaving little to the imagination from the way it hugged his body.

He was taller than Alexander, but also leaner. Where I could imagine Alexander spending hours in the gym, lifting heavy weights and doing all those grueling workouts, this man in front of me reminded me of a swimmer.

But he had no mask on his face.

I could see every sharp line, the mischievous glint in his eyes, and those eyebrows slightly darker than his hair, casting a shadow over his dark eyes.

"I'm okay," I answered and stepped closer to the railing, feeling the wind on my skin. "But thank you for asking."

"I don't think we have met." He again stepped closer. I knew that if he decided to come all the way to me, I would have nowhere to run.

I didn't know these people. I couldn't know if one of them was a crazed maniac or if they really were good and honest people.

But I knew the face of the man in front of me, and it wasn't because I saw him on a billboard somewhere, or because he was just another CEO or famous person.

I knew him because his family and mine had spent summers together on the coast of Alfenghar. I knew him because the last time I saw him, he told me I had the prettiest eyes he had ever seen and that he liked the seashells I found on the shore.

Dominic Talon stood in front of me like a ghost from the past, but he couldn't recognize me thanks to the mask I was wearing.

Or at least he didn't show that he did.

"I am—"

"I know who you are," I blurted out, squeezing my eyes shut as soon as the words left my mouth.

"Do you now?" He smirked, completely clueless about the battle going on inside of me.

Did I tell him? Did I keep it a secret?

It wasn't his fault that he forgot about me, but seeing him here felt like a bad dream. All those happy memories I stored somewhere in the chest of wonders reserved for things I didn't want to think about were about to tumble outside.

It was easier living without those happy memories because those were what haunted you the most.

And for me, those were the last memories I had of my parents.

Some days I thought I was forgetting them. It was getting harder and harder to remember what my mom's voice sounded like, or what my dad's smile looked like. Dominic was a slap I needed to remember them all.

But this wasn't the time or place. The last thing I wanted to happen tonight was to fall apart in front of these people.

The Dominic I knew was a thirteen-year-old kid. Even though he was six years older than me, he never made it seem as if I bothered him, but I knew I had.

"I mean, you're not wearing a mask." I chuckled nervously, gripping the rail with my right hand. "It is rather easy recognizing you guys."

Our fathers grew up together—we practically grew up together—and he probably forgot all about me.

A logical part of my brain knew that there was no way he could've recognized me. The last time I saw him I was a seven-year-old girl, collecting seashells and laughing at every silly joke he told me. But the illogical part didn't care that more than ten years had passed.

It hurt being forgotten. It hurt knowing that you were truly and utterly all alone in the world.

It hurt that none of them tried to find me and my brother. If they had, I wouldn't be standing here. By the time they had managed to contact my grandparents after my parents died, Marcus and I were already lost in the foster system.

But the Talon family lived in the same city where my parents were murdered, and they did nothing. If that didn't speak volumes, I had no idea what did.

"You're Dominic Talon," I blabbered, suppressing the hurt and pain threatening to lace my words as I uttered his name. "Sorry." I lifted my hands and untied the little string holding my mask in place. "It's only fair for you to see my face."

As I lifted my head, mask-free, the gasp that escaped him didn't go unnoticed.

"My name is Echo." I stepped closer to him, masking my features. "Echo Winslow."

"Winslow?" he asked, his eyebrows furrowing. There was anger in those eyes, confusion as well. That little spark of hope lit up inside of my chest, telling me that he might have recognized me as well.

"It is nice to meet you, Echo." He shook my hand and that hope burning inside of me died a slow death. "I must say that I know almost everyone here, but I have never seen you."

That terrible crashing sound? That was my heart shattering on the floor between us.

"Yes, well…" I swallowed the tears slowly announcing themselves and stepped back. "This is the first time that I'm coming to this party."

"Dom?" Alexander's voice pulled my attention from Dominic to him. I would've been lying if I said that it didn't bring me relief. "What are you doing here?" he asked leisurely.

"I'm introducing myself to our guest here. I saw you two earlier but what can I say?" He shrugged. "I was curious."

Alexander's eyes flickered from Dominic to me as if he was asking me if I was okay. And I was. Somehow I was.

It hurt being forgotten, but it was better than Dominic giving me pitiful eyes tonight.

"I was just telling Dominic that I knew him. Well, that I know of him. Of course, I have never met him before."

I could feel Dominic's eyes on me, but I refused to look at him. He was just another reminder of everything I'd lost and this night wasn't reserved for grief. This was my rebirth, my last night in Ignis, and pain had no place here tonight.

But try telling that to my head and my heart.

A beast found its home on top of my chest, and all the warm and fuzzy feelings I'd been having completely evaporated, disappearing into thin air. My hand pressed against my chest, rubbing against my breastbone, as if I could find a release by redirecting the pain from my mind to my body.

I hated feeling like this, so completely out of balance, but I couldn't help it.

It was silly getting hurt over such stupid things, but the logical part of my mind decided to exclude itself from this conversation, leaving me breathless in the presence of my past colliding with my future.

This night was supposed to be my reincarnation. I promised myself I would live. I would do everything my brother would've done if he had lived long enough, but I didn't expect to get hit by this onslaught of emotions.

There was thunder flashing in Dominic's eyes. He wore a carefree expression, but eyes never lied. People were right when they said that you could see one's soul through their eyes, and I could see the violence waking up in Dominic. Whether it was me or something I had said, I had no idea, but I didn't like the look.

He strolled in oozing confidence, carefree, trying to introduce himself to me, and whatever it was that he saw shattered that careful illusion he had tried to present. Maybe he too recognized me but refused to acknowledge the elephant in the room.

Maybe I reminded him of something else. Maybe this Dominic was so far removed from the boy I used to know that whatever image of him I had in my mind was just a mirage.

Alexander still stood at the entrance, holding two glasses of champagne, his eyes observing both Dominic and me. I, on the other hand, focused on Alexander's bowtie, ignoring the fire burning in the pit of my stomach.

I couldn't break down. Not here and not now.

"It was definitely nice meeting you, Echo," Dominic grunted, his voice a velvety touch on my skin. "Alex." He turned to him, giving me his profile. "A word, please."

He gave me a small smile that didn't quite reach his eyes. As much as I didn't want to admit it, this cold version of Dominic gutted me. The stitches over my heart ripped open, reopening the wound I›d worked so hard to close all these years ago. The sudden need to just jump off this ship and go back into hiding rocked my entire body. Alexander's apologetic smile as he placed the champagne flutes on one of the benches in front of him only made it worse.

Cold, vehement hands of destiny wrapped themselves around my throat, and the words and smiles I wanted to give him were lost on me. There was nothing I could say. I feared that once I opened my mouth, it wouldn't be words tumbling out of me, but vicious sobs that were teetering somewhere on the edge of my sanity right now.

I needed them gone. Both of them.

Dominic didn't exactly wait for me to say anything. He didn't even wait for Alexander, as if he couldn't get away from me fast enough.

But I'd be fine.

I'd survived without any of them. Just because Dominic didn't remember me and for whatever reason didn't want to stay to meet me all over again, didn't mean that I wouldn›t be okay.

This sadness couldn't fucking last forever. Other people weren't in charge of my destiny anymore. I was.

I was the captain of my boat and tonight was my rebirth.

Curiosity was what brought me here, but the need for something new, something forbidden and uninhibited, was what kept me going when I started walking down the docks. It was only fitting that Samhain would be the night of my death and my rebirth.

chapter five

ECHO

MY NIGHTMARES BLED INTO THIS PURGATORY I CALLED life, shattering the carefully painted picture I'd tried to portray. I'd tried so fucking hard to run away from the memories, wishing for one night to be different from all the other godforsaken dark and tumultuous eves when my ribs felt too small for my lungs, pressing into the flesh, cutting off my oxygen.

I'd wanted to change the core of my being, running and running and running from everything I used to be and everything I used to do, but one look at Dominic, and it all fell apart like a house of cards, destroying the illusion.

I'd gripped the Swiss pocketknife harder, letting the edges bite into my skin, hoping that the pain in my body would take away the pain in my mind.

I was fucking forgotten.

Like I never meant anything to anyone.

It was all in vain. All these years spent in misery, hoping that one day I would be able to escape who I was and everything I did.

Every fucking thing I did was useless because this moment tonight was what I should've waited for.

That look on his face. That indescribable apathy bleeding through every pore of his body, and he didn't recognize me. I was older, yes, but I still looked like that little kid who followed him everywhere he went, because that kid... that stupid, stupid kid believed that he hung the stars up in the sky.

That kid believed that fairytales existed and that Prince Charming didn't need to rescue her, because she already had the perfect life.

And just like every single one of these people that were now exiting the boat as we docked at the small wharf, I lived in the ivory tower, oblivious to the pain and misery in our world. I was oblivious to those less fortunate than I was at the time, but I'd learned.

I had to learn if I wanted to survive the crazed eyes of those that were tasked to protect me, to keep me alive. I had to learn even when their touch made my skin crawl and my eyes tear up. At a young age, I knew that they weren't supposed to touch me like that.

I'd adapted, and I wasn't that little girl anymore.

That Echo didn't exist anymore, and Dominic Talon would find out what it meant to be afraid. All of them would see that the nightmares weren't just stories told to little children to scare them from forbidden places.

Nightmares lived inside of me, and standing here, on this motherfucking boat, I knew what I had to do. I wanted to avoid it. I wanted to simply enjoy, but they didn't deserve to live when everybody else died even though they could help.

None of these people deserved to live a life of privilege. They did nothing to gain it.

These spoiled little children of men and women who could've changed the world, didn't deserve to laugh, drink and love, when the people like me, like little Lorelei, went through life filled with rage, pain and all the bad and vile things that could exist.

These people didn't deserve mercy. Where was the mercy for me? Where were all the self-righteous men and women when my throat went raw from screaming so hard? Where were the neighbors when a little boy died?

Where the fuck were they?

The murmur of voices as they all disembarked from the boat irritated me, but I could hold my tongue. I could hold my temper in check long enough to plan, to observe, and to see what I could do to right the wrongs. I would introduce them to the misery so great that no amount of money would ever again mean anything to them.

Living on the edge of sanity always felt like a horrible way to live, but I should've known that life would always find a way to guide me where I was supposed to be.

I looked to my left, toward the coastal line of the island.

The tree line covered the entire coastline, and only a small portion, where the pathway leading from the wharf toward the road illuminated by the lamps, wasn't covered with trees. I couldn't see the mansion from here, but I had no doubt in my mind that it looked exquisite.

I couldn't wait to see its walls covered in blood.

"Echo?" A deep, dark voice called out to me and I turned around to see Alexander standing at the door. I wanted to like him. I almost allowed myself to do it. But knowing that he belonged to these people and that he played the same games as them didn't sit well with me.

And that message... I wanted to laugh out loud. They thought they could lure me here with a pretty dress and do whatever the fuck they wanted to.

We'd all heard stories about Quell Island and the poor, young women who were given one chance, one night, to live the life they always dreamed of having.

Whoever had sent it had no idea who they were inviting to their little soiree. They had no idea that the Devil often looked like lost, young girls, waiting to be swept off their feet. And even though I wanted that, I wanted happiness and love, it wasn't going to happen tonight.

It definitely wasn't going to happen with any of these people.

"Everyone is leaving the boat," Alexander continued when I just kept staring at him. "Are you ready to go?"

My hands itched both from the need to touch him, to forget

what every nerve ending in my body screamed at me to do, and from the need to open this knife and to stab him in his heart.

Losing myself to the primal instincts wouldn't bode well for me, and instead, I lifted my dress and tucked the knife back into its place.

I didn't miss the way Alexander's eyes focused on my bare legs, nor the flaring of his nostrils as I lifted my dress higher and higher. Maybe it was the anger seeping through the cracks, but I wanted to play.

I kept my eyes on him, drinking every smooth line, every muscle straining against his tuxedo, and repositioned myself on the bench, fully facing him. My dress was already on top of my thighs, but it wasn't enough.

I wanted him to lose control.

I wanted them all to lose control, to go wild, insane, just like me. I yearned to feel him tremble under my hands, to feel his energy mingling with mine.

Spreading my legs, I pulled the tulle fabric higher and higher, until it rested around my hips. My fingers danced on the bare skin of my legs, touching and taunting, breaking that stubborn line on his forehead as he kept watching.

"What are you doing?" Alexander asked, his voice guttural, matching the fire burning in my veins.

Throwing my head back, I let the hoodie fall off my head, freeing my hair for the first time tonight. "I'm playing a game," I whispered, only loud enough for him to hear. "Would you like to play with me?" I let the question roll off my tongue as I looked at him.

"Echo," he all but growled, taking a small step forward as if he wasn't in control of his own body.

His hands flexed, fighting for control, but I didn't want control. Not tonight.

"Play with me, Alexander," I purred. "Come," I called for him and removed the jacket from my shoulders.

"Stop it," he bit out, but the resolve was slowly disappearing from his eyes. He might have wanted to be a better person than me, but there was no denying that he wanted me just as much as I wanted him.

"Please," I moaned as I pressed my fingers against my clit, rubbing it in circles. My panties covered me from his eyes, but the wetness pooling from my core as I rocked against my hand would soon destroy them. "I need you," I murmured, and that was all it took.

Seconds barely passed before he crossed the small distance between us, positioning himself between my legs. His face was aligned with my crotch, but I couldn't see his expression because of that fucking mask.

"Remove the mask," I pleaded. "Please."

The tick in his jaw was prominent, but he did what I asked. With smooth movements, he untied the ribbon and pulled the mask off his face.

If I thought he was stunning before, it was nothing compared to fully seeing him.

Dark eyebrows cast a shadow over his pale, blue eyes that were getting darker and darker with every passing second. His expression was one of hunger, of need mirroring my own, and no matter how this started or why I did this, I wanted this man.

I lifted my other hand, slowly, so fucking slowly, as if he would bolt if I rushed any of my movements, and pressed it against his cheek, almost giggling as his stubble tickled my palm.

"You're beautiful," I breathed out, stroking his cheek with my thumb.

His eyes fluttered closed, leaning into my touch. If it wasn't for the wickedness hanging above our heads, I would've enjoyed this moment a lot more. But softness didn't have a place here tonight. It wasn't invited to this funeral for souls. As if he knew, he pushed my hand away from my pussy and dove, inhaling my scent.

Alexander gripped my knee with his other hand and pushed it further apart. His teeth clamped down on my now soaked panties, pulling them away from my feverish skin. There was an inferno fighting to escape me.

Energy cracked between us as he ripped my panties off my body and pulled my knees over his shoulders.

I knew what was about to come, but I never expected the jolt I would get as he lapped at my folds, feasting on me like a man starved. His tongue ran from my clit to my opening, while his hands gripped my thighs.

For years I'd tried to extinguish that fire that burned deep inside of my core, but I did such a fucked-up job that it felt as if I was pouring oil on it instead of water. I should've realized that killing who you were never worked out for anyone.

It only ever appeased people around you while your soul crumbled and cried, miserable in the little bubble you were trying to contain it in.

And mine… mine couldn't be contained. Not anymore.

"Fuck!" I yelled out, uncaring that there were people who could probably hear me. Uncaring that they could see us if they came to this side of the boat, or that the time kept ticking and we were probably the last two people on the boat.

I couldn't give a fuck about any of that. As the fire licked my skin as Alexander licked, bit, and soothed my burning flesh, I climbed higher and higher, gripping his hair, both pushing him away and pulling him closer.

He replaced his tongue with his fingers, stroking and pinching, pulling me closer to him, until his fingers entered effortlessly, sliding inside my slick channel.

"We shouldn't be doing this," he panted against my lips as he lifted himself up. "But fuck if I care at the moment."

His lips crashed against mine, fighting for dominance, looking for surrender. But he wasn't going to get it from me.

I moved my hips in the rhythm of his fingers, needing more of him, more of this insane pull I'd felt from the first moment my eyes connected with his. His teeth clamped down on my lower lip, eliciting a small whimper from me, but he never stopped pushing me toward the edge.

My breathing quickened, my heartbeat erratic, and all I could see, all I could think about, were his fingers inside of me and the insane need to let go. Just to fucking let go.

"Alex," I hissed.

"I know, darling," he mumbled against my cheek. "I know."

"I need to… I-I… Fuck!"

"Let it go, Sparrow. Give it to me." He pressed his lips against my cheek, trailing a path all the way to my ear. "I want to hear you scream for me."

"Fuuuuuck!"

My hips bucked, the tingling sensation in the pit of my stomach turning into a full-blown volcano erupting from my body.

"I-I'm," I stuttered. "Alex!" I gripped his hair, holding him close to me as his fingers went in and out, pushing, pushing, and pushing, brushing against that sweet, forbidden spot inside of my channel. "I can't!"

"Yes, you can," he grunted. "Scream, Echo. I want them to hear you. I want them to know what a filthy little girl you are."

Something tore inside of my chest. Cracked open. Vulnerable.

It was something I hadn't felt in forever, but it felt good. It felt right.

As my throat went hoarse, and my body went slack in Alexander's eyes, I looked over his shoulder to see Dominic standing at the door, looking at us with disgust in his eyes.

I should've been embarrassed. I should've moved from Alexander. But as he stood there, fuming, looking at me as if I was less than gum on the sole of his shoes, I smirked.

We were playing my game now.

chapter six

DOMINIC

MISERY LOVES COMPANY, OR AT LEAST THAT'S WHAT people often said

My misery was the woman that looked so much like the little girl that followed me everywhere I went. All this time, I thought she was dead.

But could it be her? Could it be my Echo Selke?

The last time I saw her she had pigtails and a red polka dot dress, showing me all the seashells she managed to collect on the beach in front of the hotel we were all staying at. Had it already been ten years since the last time I saw her?

How was it possible that I forgot all about her?

Our families were extremely close, to the point where our mothers joked about me marrying Echo one day, until it all went up in flames and her family... it wasn't possible. No.

The entire Selke family died that night. That's what they told me, dammit.

My skin felt too tight, pressing in on my bones, cutting off the oxygen I needed. As I climbed toward the main road from the wharf, I wondered if I could really do this tonight. I promised Kairos I would, but seeing that girl...

"Good evening, sir," a driver greeted me as I hurried toward the car. The driver opened the door for me seconds before I reached them.

I fucking hated all of this, but I played along.

I had no other choice.

They were watching, expecting us to fail. Expecting us to go back, crawling to them, to beg them for forgiveness and mercy, but they weren't going to get either of those from us.

The sleek, black seats smelled of leather, choking me, reminding me of all those nights spent inside—

No. I shook my head, willing those memories to go away. This was one night where the three of us could be who we really were. One night in the entire year where I didn't have to hide behind the perfectly curated mask of control and calmness.

Tonight I could be wild, free, careless, and seeing that girl who resembled little Echo and had her name wouldn't knock me off my feet. But the resemblance was eerie. Those eyes, the same midnight black hair, could it really be her?

If it was, did she really forget about me or was she pretending?

"Should we go directly to the Manor, sir?" the driver asked from the front seat as I stewed over what happened tonight. I didn't want to be surrounded by these people, but both Kairos and Alexander were going to be there. If I didn't show up, they would send their bloodhounds to look for me. I didn't have it in me yet to start causing unnecessary mayhem.

"To the Manor, please," I mumbled, turning my head toward the window as the car started.

It would've been better if I didn't.

Alexander appeared at the side of the road, gripping her hand in his. I should've thrown him into the water for what he did tonight. He shouldn't have touched her.

None of us were allowed to touch her until the witching hour, and he already managed to fuck it all up. If Kairos found out...

But he doesn't have to find out, my subconscious piped in. He never has to know, and you can play with her too.

My fist connected with the seat in front of me, "Fuck!" The drive didn't even blink. I guess that working for Kairos Adair meant that nothing ever fazed you.

"Sorry," I grumbled, clearing my throat.

"It's okay, sir. Master Adair has everything ready. I'm sure you will be able to relax once we are at the Manor."

I highly doubted that.

These events were starting to grate on my nerves. As each year passed, I feared that we were getting further away from the final goal. Instead of finding her, we'd spent years fucking through the girls that came through the Manor. But none of them were what we were looking for.

Not one of them would've been able to withstand everything that the Infernal Triumvirate meant.

But that girl on the boat, Echo... There was something in her eyes that I hadn›t seen before.

The violence, the defiance, as if she knew something I didn't. Whether or not she was the little Echo from all those years ago, there was so much misery hiding in those blue orbs. But when she looked at me as Alexander hugged her, my cock stirred to life and I fucking hated it.

The fact that I wanted to smash Alexander's head against the bench didn't help to settle the feeling in my gut. I wished it was because I was simply jealous, but it was more than that.

He should've called me. He shouldn't have done this.

Ten million should haves and I had no idea how Kairos was going to take this. We had to let him know.

"Five more minutes, sir," the driver spoke again, pulling me back from the miserable thoughts swirling inside my head.

The wharf wasn't too far away from the Manor, but I never refused an opportunity to bitch about the fact that we all had to come with that fucking boat that took forever driving us back and forth. All those pompous pricks vying for my attention, and all those girls all but throwing themselves at me and my friends were getting tiring.

Years ago, all of this was exciting, new, something that the three of us had created without the help of our families, but now... Now it all felt shallow, useless. I couldn't shake the unease in the pit of my stomach.

The forest surrounded the Manor and covered the majority of the island. As we passed through the tall, iron gates, I braced myself for the incessant chattering throughout the night I would have to suffer through, until the main event.

I never understood why we had to tolerate the useless mingling with the other patrons, when they all knew what they were getting into.

Well, all of them except for the Maiden.

A smile pulled at my face, knowing that by the end of the night, that defiant little smirk she sent my way would be wiped away from her face. I would break her, make her submit to me—to us—until she understood that the only gods she would worship from now on were the ones from the Infernal Triumvirat.

Alexander was too soft for that. Kairos... Kairos was a motherfucking psychopath who wouldn't mind killing them if that was what it took. But me, I liked to take my sweet time. Their fear tasted better than any other aphrodisiac, and I bet that Echo tasted exquisite.

"We're here, Mr. Talon," the old man driving announced as we stopped in front of the main entrance to the Manor. The butlers stood at the main door, greeting the guests who kept spilling out of their own cars.

I hated every single one of them.

Kairos was no doubt already waiting inside, expecting us all to go to him, but I would let him mingle with his little minions before I even attempted to talk to him.

I opened the door of the car, unable to wait another second, as the valet kept opening the door of all the cars in front of us and strolled over the gravel road toward the entrance door.

"Welcome back, Mr. Talon." One of the waitresses smiled at me, extending the tray filled with drinks toward me. I knew her from last year, and the twinkle in her eyes said that she wanted a repeat of the performance from back then.

Not going to happen.

Grimly, I nodded at her and took a champagne glass from the second girl who kept avoiding my eyes, and strolled inside of the Manor.

I laughed when Kairos told us about this place for the first time. His father got it as a gift—or at least that's what he called it—and decided to let it rot while he traveled all over the world with his girlfriends and friends. Kairos refurbished the place, bringing it to what it was today.

He turned this haunted place into a home, an escape for us. Even though I hated October thirty-first with a passion, I couldn't hate this house.

But the fact that Kairos and Alexander kept insisting to hold this motherfucking ball every single year somehow tarnished this place in my eyes. I tried to steer clear from here the rest of the year, preferring to meet with them somewhere in the city. But there was a weird kind of electricity running amok tonight, and I wanted to see what would happen.

Things went more than wrong last year, and we had to make up for all the lost time.

The last time I saw Kairos was five months ago when I told him to fuck off. But he did tell me about the girl. He told me about the perfect girl that could be our final—

"Dom." A high-pitched voice wrapped around my throat, annoying me even before I saw the familiar face as I turned around.

Anastasia fucking Dawson.

Ethereal beauty and a rotten soul went hand in hand, and she was a prime example of everything that was wrong with society. Her eyelashes fluttered as she looked up at me, expecting… what? A hug?

"Hi, Anastasia," I grumbled, looking around me.

"It's been a long time," she purred, placing her hand on my chest. There was a time, not so long ago, where having the attention of a pretty woman like her meant I was the king of the world. Not anymore.

I saw them all for what they were. All these serpents danced among angels, waiting for their final fall. And I fell.

Oh, how I fell.

And this bitch standing in front of me, with her fake eyelashes, shiny hair, and a new set of boobs, was the first one to sell me out. To sell my friends out.

"What are you doing here?" I asked her, enjoying the way she squirmed. She fucked us all up, shattering the dream we all had.

"Don't be like that." She swatted my hand. "Kairos invited me." Her saccharine smile made me sick. The fact that she thought something good would come out of this for her made the hair at the nape of neck stand up.

I narrowed my eyes on her. "Kairos?" I was going to throw him into the pool. "When did this happen?"

"Just the other day. He came to the premiere of Just Another Boy and gave me an invitation."

"Kairos?" I asked again, sounding like a parrot to myself.

Her eyes rolled, annoyance as clear as the day on her face. "Yes, Dom." She huffed. "Kairos invited me. He told me he missed seeing me."

Or he missed fucking her.

Whatever the case, I could see that there was something he wasn't telling me. Something that would most likely piss me off.

But whatever it was wouldn't piss me off more than seeing Alexander walking inside the Manor with Echo clutching his arm. She looked like a Goddess in a floor-length dress pooling around her feet, and that corset that accentuated her figure. Her mask was a stark contrast to the rest of her outfit, including her hair. It wasn't until her eyes froze on me that I stopped listening to whatever it was that Anastasia said.

The defiance in her gaze, the anger, I yearned to fuck it all out of her, to make it known that she had no power here.

After that first conversation, I expected her to be afraid, to tremble or to run away. Instead, she walked as if she owned the place, looking at the rest of the people as if they were mere peasants only placed here to please her. Alexander walked as if he had just conquered the world, and I wanted to wipe away that smug smile.

"Are you even listening to me, Dom?" God, her voice grated on my nerves.

"Anastasia." I looked down at her and gulped the champagne

I'd been holding. "Just shut the fuck up and try not to end up dead." I handed her the glass.

The other guests mingled, talked, laughed, and chatted with each other, half of them unaware of what was going to happen tonight. The other half—they were checking out their competition. Frankly, I couldn't give a fuck what any of them did tonight if I managed to get my hands on the girl that seemed to be annoyed by my very presence.

I could see her hair billowing behind her as they walked toward the ballroom, and the moth tattoo taking over half of her back, almost looked alive as her muscles moved.

Her face might have seemed young, but the wickedness I could see in the mirror every fucking day was also hiding there in her eyes, waiting to be released. Her shoulders were tense, her right hand flexing at her hip, and fucking Alexander didn't think to take her somewhere else first.

I shouldn't care about her. I shouldn't want to take her away from all these people, just to make her comfortable. She was prey and nothing more, but God, something inside my chest roared with the need to protect her.

Even if it meant protecting her from us.

"Alex!" I yelled out, stopping them in their tracks. If her shoulders were tense before, it was nothing compared to her body language now. She wanted to appear unfazed, calm and collected, but the truth hid in the lines of her face or at least what I could see of it, and the flat line of her lips.

"We need to talk," I murmured to Alex, completely ignoring

her. "And we need to find Kairos. There are some things we need to discuss." I allowed myself one look at her, at the smooth, pale skin and the way she held herself.

"Seriously," Alexander hissed, looking around us. "I thought that we closed this topic."

"It's not that topic." I looked back at him, fighting the urge to reach out to her, to run my fingers over her collarbone all the way to her full lips. "There's something else. Something you should know as well."

"Now?"

"Yes, right fucking now." I was losing my patience, and I knew that it had nothing to do with the way Alex spoke to me. "Get your ass moving." I started walking away from them. "Alone, Alexander."

"Fuck off, Dom!" he yelled after me.

Gladly, but I had to stay here.

chapter seven

ECHO

CRYSTAL CHANDELIERS AND PORCELAIN FUCKING hearts—that's what was in store for me tonight, But if anything, I loved seeing that annoyed look on Dominic's face. Unlike the rest of us, he didn't wear his mask, and it reminded me of a young Dom who never really cared for rules.

I guess it was easy not following them when the entire world lay in the palm of your hand, and you could do whatever the fuck you wanted to.

Must have been nice living in a glass box, safe from the outside world. No rules and no consequences.

The air conditioning made this place colder than the mountair

Athros in the middle of December. But my jacket didn't exactly go along with the dress I was wearing, and instead of carrying it with me, I gave it to the guys at the entrance, exposing myself to the sharks circling around me.

One of them had it out for me tonight it would seem.

Anastasia was talking to Dominic when we came in, and I couldn't stop the gleeful feeling when I saw him stepping away from her, annoyed with whatever it was that she was saying.

I could feel her eyes on me. When I tried escaping her and her group of friends by going to the furthest part of the ballroom, they still followed me with their eyes, no doubt whispering about the unknown girl standing alone.

My eyes scanned the crowd. For the first time, I saw that not every single person belonged to high society. Some of them kept looking around as if they weren't supposed to be here, but the grips those men and women had on their arms were indication enough that some of them didn't even want to be here.

Which pissed me off even more.

I had no idea what this gathering was about or why that invitation found its way to my room, but as time passed, I could feel it more and more in my gut—I was supposed to be here.

I looked at the group of women standing a few feet away from me, mentioning Kairos Adair and his two friends, but I had yet to see this infamous man. Alexander and Dominic were obviously the two friends, but Kairos was nowhere to be seen.

Wasn't this his party?

"So," a feminine voice sounded behind me and as I turned around. It was one of Anastasia's friends. "I didn't quite get your name?" Her fake smile made me sick to my stomach.

"Because I never gave it to you," I retorted, sipping the vodka cranberry I got from the bar.

Her smile wobbled, and she kept glancing back at her group. "But you need to tell us your name. Mine is—"

"I don't care." I looked at her. "Whatever game you guys are trying to play won't work. Now go back to your little friends and tell them to fuck off."

Her eyes widened, shock and disbelief visible even behind the blue mask she wore. "B-But… You can't—"

"What? Tell you to fuck off?" I smiled. "You really should find better friends, darling. You don't want to fuck with me. Trust me."

If only they knew.

"Where are you going?" she called out after me as I started walking toward the tall, glass doors. "Hey!" Her heels clicked against the floor, but I was faster with my boots.

I didn't have enough patience to deal with her and also pretend that I wanted to be here.

The cold air slammed into me as soon as I stepped through the doors, lower even than the coldness they were creating on the inside.

"Jeez." I shivered, rubbing my arm with my free hand. "Is it fucking December already?" I asked out loud to no one in particular and walked to the end of the balcony where another set of stairs led toward the ground.

A large, already covered pool stood in front of me as I climbed down. If I wasn't that distracted by the stunning bush of red roses right next to the pool, I would've noticed a lone figure standing on the other side.

My fingers froze as I reached out toward the roses, my eyes glued to the man whose face I couldn't see. But I fucking knew those shoulders and the shape of that body.

Even in the shadows, I would've been able to recognize him no matter how many years had passed.

I placed the now empty glass on one of the sun loungers and started walking toward him. I needed to see him. I had to know if the connection I felt on that rooftop was just a figment of my imagination or if it was something tangible, something I could hold on to.

I needed him to block all those other thoughts away.

"We finally meet, little Sparrow."

Fuck. Me.

His voice felt like velvet on my cold skin. As he stepped into the light, the breath I was about to take lodged itself in my throat. My lips were dry, parched, suddenly thirsty for something more than simply water.

His jet-black hair swayed with the wind and curled around his face. As the light illuminated his entire body, I took a step back, seeing that he didn't wear a mask like the rest of us.

Instead, skull makeup was masterfully applied to his skin, hiding the real person. Who the fuck was he?

"I would probably say the same, but I have no idea who you

are," I said with renewed strength, surprised at the tone of my voice.

Even with the distance between us, I could feel the raw, unhinged power emanating from him. I knew that it was him. The same animalistic attraction that I'd had for the simple shadow slammed into me in full force, pushing me one step backward.

Where everyone else wore tuxedos and suits, this man wore a white shirt, tucked into a black pants that were hugging his thighs. Rolled-up sleeves at his forearms revealed tattoos I didn't have time to investigate, but I wanted to.

I wanted to walk toward him, to tell him that I'd waited long enough, but my pride and the stupidity of yesterday haunted me, stopping me from doing it.

His long legs ate the distance between us. Before I could turn away and leave him just as he left me so many times in the past, he stopped right in front of me, taking my hand in his.

"You know who I am, Echo. You've always known."

I kept my eyes plastered on the black buttons on his shirt, avoiding his eyes. "I'm afraid that I have no idea what you are talking about."

"Hmm," he grumbled and placed his finger beneath my chin, forcing me to look up. "I think you're fucking lying, Sparrow."

His eyes were the darkest eyes I had ever seen. The irises almost blended with the dark brown color around, and if it wasn't for golden specs breaking the darkness in them, I would've thought that they were black.

"Who are you?" I whispered, afraid that loud talking would

destroy this tiny bubble we were in right now.

"I am the reason you are here. Well…" he chuckled. "Me and my friends actually, but you've already met them."

"I did?"

"Oh yes." He frowned. "Especially Alexander."

Shit.

Shit. Fuck. Shit.

"You're Kairos Adair." It wasn't a question, but a statement. As if he burned me instead of soothing the darkness swirling in my veins, I stepped back, regretting it almost instantly when the freezing wind slammed into me.

"Why did that sound more like an accusation than relief?"

Because I would have to kill you now, I almost said. Because I would need to tear your heart apart, and that would kill mine too.

"Sorry." I smiled at him, hoping to mask the disappointment tainting the memories of the last couple of months. "I think I'm just tired."

"You didn't go anywhere else last night," he said. It should've chilled me to the bone that he wasn't saying it as a question.

"Did you follow me?" I narrowed my eyes on him. "Why?"

"Because." He came closer again, lowering his head down until his nose pressed against my hair. "I needed to know you were safe."

"That's called stalking."

"Not if it wasn't me that was following you."

"Tomato, tomahto, it's the same shit," I hissed. "You sent me the invitation as well?"

"How else would I be able to get you here?"

"Why?" I asked again, needing to know the answer. "You've spent months watching me, and not once did you approach me."

"I wasn't the only one watching you, little Sparrow. They did too." He looked over my shoulder. As I turned around, I saw Alexander and Dominic walking toward us.

"Although, I must admit, there were times where I wanted you all to myself. But Alexander saw you before I could decide what exactly it was that I wanted to do with you, and it was done."

"What the fuck are you talking about?" I looked from him to Dominic to Alexander, who wore the same painted makeup as him. "Alex." I looked at him. "What is he talking about?"

"We've been searching for a Maiden for a very long time, but no one has ever fit the role as well as you," Kairos answered instead. His chest pressed against my back. With Dominic and Alexander in front of me, I knew I had nowhere to run.

Think, Echo. Think, dammit.

"Welcome to the Triumvirat, Sparrow."

"W-what ar—"

That's when I felt it, the stinging pain in my neck, the weakness in my body as he pushed whatever was in the syringe. As my legs stopped cooperating, Kairos wrapped his arm around my waist, holding me close to him.

"What have you done?" I looked at him, before I fell into oblivion.

chapter eight

KAIROS

HER DARK HAIR TICKLED MY ARM, SPILLING OVER IT as I carried her inside of the Manor, avoiding the gazes of people gathered on the balcony. I could hear Alexander and Dominic whispering behind me, displeased with the way I handled the situation. But tonight had to be different from all the other Halloween Eves. It was now or never and we all had something to prove.

All these people invited here were just a coverup for the real thing. They were pawns I used to mask what was really going on. This girl in my arms, this extraordinary creature would be ours—one way or another.

The first time I saw her on the cameras in my building, I thought I was seeing a ghost. She seemed so tiny in comparison to me, so fragile, but the moment she started dancing, I forgot that I wanted to kick her out.

I thought she was just another homeless person looking for a place to crash for the night, but she wasn't.

From that first moment when my eyes followed her every move, I knew she had to be ours. There were no words strong enough to describe the war waging inside of me when she looked at me, even though I knew she couldn't see my face.

Alexander and Dominic often said that I was a cold and callous bastard, always thinking, planning, calculating my every move, but she... she wasn't a part of my plan.

Up until that moment, the old tale we were told was nothing but a story told by those that came before us. A miserable excuse to have that kind of a relationship like previous members of the Triumvirat that some girl could be the glue holding the three members together. I went along, because no matter what I was still a superstitious bastard, but I never intended to keep any of them.

None of them made my blood boil.

Not one of them made my cock as hard as steel, pushing against my trousers, by simply showing their real faces. And this girl, our girl, wore her heart on her sleeve. Every movement of her body as she danced represented parts of her that she kept hidden from other people.

Even tonight, as she entered the Manor with Alex in tow, she looked like she already owned the place. Like a true Queen, a ruler in its making. God, I wanted to take all three of them and take them far away from here.

But there was a ritual that needed to be done, and judging by the look on her face, she wouldn't exactly be all too willing to give us what we wanted.

But it was okay. I could break her. I knew that Dominic itched to do so as well. This defiant siren that clutched to me even in her unconscious state would either be our beginning or our end.

We were yet to see which one would prevail.

"Where are you taking her?" Dominic asked from behind me. I didn't miss the strain in his voice, the madness tethering on the edges of sanity and his insatiable hunger for destruction.

"To her room," I answered, instead of dwelling on what had gotten into him tonight. He'd been on edge ever since I told him about her a couple of days ago. If he thought that he could avoid talking to me about the things that bothered him forever, he had another think coming. "We need to get her ready for tonight."

I expected him to protest, to say that he didn't want to do this. It was there in his eyes, in the way he avoided Alex and me, but he didn't say a thing. Dominic simply fell in line, like he always did, but something about this time bothered me.

Stopping abruptly, I turned toward them, seeing as we were all alone now in the east wing of the Manor, and looked at them— really, really looked at them.

They were my best friends, my blood brothers, the reason I agreed to do this in the first place. All three of us came from wealthy families, but also families that hid their skeletons in their perfect little closets—flawless in the eyes of the public, yet rotten to the core behind closed doors.

We saved each other in a way and committed to this insanity when we agreed to form a new Infernal Triumvirat. It sounded insane just talking about it, but the previous Triumvirat found us when we were in our early twenties, starved for attention, for power, for anything that could help us forget the insanity we went through as kids.

I was the oldest one at twenty-seven, Alexander just three years younger than me. Dominic was the baby of the group, barely twenty-three, and he worried me the most. The descent into hell was paved with good intentions, and more often than not, those good intentions landed us in the purgatory we didn't know we were entering.

The scars he hid on his body, covered by tattoos, were proof enough that those who presented themselves as perfect, God-fearing families were the demons in the making, waiting for the perfect opportunity to strike.

And they struck him.

"Dom," I murmured, pulling his attention back to me. "Are you sure you want to do this?" I asked, fearing what the answer would be.

I knew he was pulling away from us. Day by day, month by month, he was becoming more and more distant, disappearing for months on end, coming back ravaged by the demons he was trying to fight. But he always came back.

I feared the day he wouldn't. I feared that one day the madness pushing and probing at his mind would take over, leaving us with nothing more but a shell of a man he used to be.

"Dom," I said again when he just kept staring at Echo.

"She's beautiful," he murmured, as if he was remembering something. "She was always so beautiful, even as a kid. Pure, untouched, happy, and so full of love. We are going to destroy her."

"What are you talking about?" Alexander asked, his gaze bouncing between Echo and me and Dominic. "Do you know her?"

Dominic shrugged, his eyes never leaving Echo's sleeping face, but the torment on his face almost knocked me off my feet. I had never seen him look like this. Every other girl who came to us was nothing more but a way to pass time.

A fun, new thing we all played with, before we discarded her, giving her back to the world.

But I wanted us to keep this one, and Dominic wasn't on board with that.

"Dominic," I barked, bringing his attention back to me. His irises were shot, misery etched into every single line on his face, and I didn't know what to do. "What are you talking about, Dom?"

"I know her," he mumbled. "Or, well…" he smiled sadly. "I think I know her, or at least I used to know her."

"What are you…" I started and looked at Alexander. "What is he talking about?"

Alexander shrugged. "I have no idea, dude. He never told me."

"Her family." Dominic cleared his throat and started talking. "Her family used to hang out with mine, but they weren't good people. None of them were. I tried to save her from it all. I tried to keep her from them."

"Dominic!" I thundered. "Start making sense for fuck's sake."

"I don't know what happened!" Dominic bellowed. "But they died. They all died, and the little girl who felt like sunshine wasn't a part of my life anymore."

"So why do you think that she is this girl you're talking about?" Alexander asked him, placing a hand on his shoulder. "Hey, talk to us."

"They have the same name," Dominic mumbled and came closer to Echo and me. His hand trembled as he lifted it toward her hair. "The same hair, the same eyes… This is her. This is Echo from my childhood."

"Dom—"

"I don't know what happened to her. I only know what my fucking father told me. I don't think it was an accident."

"For fuck's sake," I hissed and turned around, storming toward the room we were going to place her in.

"Kai!" Alexander called after me. "Dude," he said as he caught up with me. "It's only Dominic. You know how he gets."

"He's never like this, not over a girl," I said as I kicked open the door and walked inside the room. "Never like this, Alex. Something's wrong with him. Something neither one of us understands, but something is fucking wrong."

"He's okay, Kai," Alexander said, as if he was trying to convince himself more than me. "He's going to be okay."

"I am okay," Dominic said as he walked inside the room. "But I'm telling you, this girl… she isn't nobody. She meant something to me back in the day."

"How are you so sure that this is the same girl?"

"I just know, okay?" He breathed out. "I know this is her. The fact that we're going to destroy her tonight doesn't sit well with me. None of this does."

Gently, I placed her on the bed, turning back to Dominic and Alex who stood in the middle of the room now. The worry etched on Alexander's face only added to my own, but we didn't have time to go over everything that Dominic was saying.

"Dominic." I approached him, taking his face in my hands. "She's not that girl, okay? She has no family. I did a background check on her. She's an orphan, living in a group home on the other side of the city. She isn't some long-lost friend of yours. Get that fucking thought out of your head."

"Then why does it feel like I know her?" he bit out and stepped back. "I know you feel it too." He looked at me. "Don't even try to deny it. Every other girl was nothing but a passing thought for all three of us, yet this one," he pointed at Echo, "she already has us wrapped around her pinky finger and she isn't even trying. I have a war inside my chest! A fucking war, where one side wants me to destroy her, to make her as filthy and as broken as I am, while the other one wants to hold her, cherish her, show her what it means to be safe."

"Dominic, it's not—" Alexander started before Dominic cut him off.

"You feel it too. Why would you do what you did on the boat, huh? She already owns us and I'm not sure that's such a good thing. Especially not right now."

"What do you mean?" I asked, narrowing my eyes on him.

"What did you do, Dom?"

Silence descended on us. Alex and I looked at each other, trying to figure out what was going on.

"I fucked up," Dominic whispered and dropped to the floor, crossing his legs as he sat down. "I did something I shouldn't have." He looked down at the floor, avoiding our eyes.

"What did you do?" I asked.

"And they found her. They shouldn't have found her. I made sure of that."

"What. Did. You. Do?" I asked through gritted teeth, hating the fact that I had no idea what happened.

"Clarissa Hutchins," he mumbled, playing with a loose string on the carpet. "The girl from last year," he continued, but I already knew what he was going to say.

We'd spent days and nights looking for her after she disappeared from the party last year. Police came and went, but no one had any answers to what happened. One moment, she was with me, agreeing to be our Maiden, and the next, she disappeared.

"Domi—"

"I killed her," he said flatly as if it was something that he never should've done. Lifting his head, he looked at Echo and then at us. "And I can't remember half of it."

"Shit," Alexander mumbled and sat down next to him.

"I didn't mean to. I think. But I hated her," he bit out. "I hated the way you two fell for her, worse than Anastasia. I hated the fact that there was no space for me in that relationship."

"Dominic—"

"No! I'm afraid that I'm going to kill her too when the darkness descends on my mind." He looked at Echo again. "That's why I'm torn. I can feel it coming, this need to destroy her, to show her how much it could really hurt, and I can't do that. Not to her when she reminds me of one person who was always kind to me."

"You're not going to hurt her," I murmured and kneeled in front of him. My hand clamped down on his shoulder, kneading the tight muscles there. "You're not the sum of your mistakes, Dominic."

"One day, I might believe you," he murmured, tracing the invisible pattern on my shirt. His other hand wrapped around my neck, and he pulled me down closer to him, closer to his lips, waiting for me, free for taking. "But today, I don't believe you. I don't know if she will be enough to put me together again."

He bit down on my lower lip, earning a grunt from me. It wasn't strong enough to break the skin, but hard enough to stir the need coiling in my gut. It'd been too long since I had him here with us. It'd been too long since I felt his hands on my skin, or his lips on mine.

As he kept gripping the back of my neck, pulling me closer and closer until he got up on his knees, pressing his chest against mine, I could feel his need.

Not only the physical one, even though his rock-hard dick pressing against mine was indication enough of where he wanted to take this. No, it was the need inside his soul that was always there for us.

The need to escape, to run away, to get lost with us even if it was only for one night. If today was any other date, I would've allowed this.

"Dom," I murmured against his lips. "We can't do this. Not yet."

"Please," he whispered, trembling against me. "I just want to forget it all. Please, take it away from me. I'm begging you, Kai. Take these memories away from me."

"He can't," a melodic voice piped in behind us. As if someone threw a bucket of cold water over us, I tore myself away from Dominic and fell on my back.

I saw her then, standing next to the bed like the Goddess of Darkness, looking at the three of us. She held herself upright with one hand on the bed, swaying on her feet, no doubt the effects of the drugs I'd given her.

It wasn't enough to knock her out for a longer period of time, but it was enough to piss her off. And boy, she was fucking pissed off. Her eyes were narrowed at the three of us, calculating, her face open as a fucking book, showing almost every single thought passing through her mind.

So much anger would suffocate a lesser person, but not her. I expected fear from her, or maybe her bolting for the door while we weren't looking. The defiance and violence seeping from her brilliant eyes weren't what I expected to see.

Yet I loved it.

My eyes drank her in—her smooth skin and the way she observed us as if we were here for her and not the other way around.

She was the missing piece of our trio. Her energy, the way she stood here, already owning us without trying. We were doomed if we continued our life without her. I knew that I couldn't let her go.

I pulled myself up, seeing the shocked expressions on the faces of my guys, yet Dominic couldn't look away from her.

"I want—" he started as she walked, no, stalked toward him, completely ignoring Alex and me. I chose her because she would've been the perfect prey for the three predators lurking in the middle of the night. I never assumed that she could be a predator herself.

"I know," she interrupted him and kneeled in front of him. "I know what you need, but you need me as much as you need them."

"I'll destroy you," Dominic said, sorrow and pain lacing every word softly spoken.

"No, Dominic," she whispered, leaning down. Her lips pressed against his cheek and her arms around him. "I am going to destroy you, and then we can all be hollow together. Maybe tonight won't be the end, but a new beginning for all of us."

chapter nine

ECHO

WE WERE ALL BROKEN, EVERY SINGLE ONE OF US. AS the grogginess cleared from my mind, slowly pulling me back to reality, I could hear the broken pleas and whispers of the man kneeling in front of me.

I hated it. It resembled my own misery, and like looking in the mirror, Dominic's feelings were as clear as mine.

The only difference was, neither one of them was a villain— that role belonged to me. And fuck if I cared what name they called me once everything was said and done. I could quiet down those miserable and weak parts of my soul that wanted to weep for three fucked-up men sitting in front of me.

Anger simmered beneath my skin, swallowing the light breaking through the windows, cast by the moon. These fucking idiots had no idea what this night meant for me. But they would learn.

They all did—eventually.

"We can't do this," Kairos said from behind me, irritating me almost immediately. "We need to do the ritual."

"Fuck the ritual," Dominic growled, pulling me closer to him. "We don't need a ritual to know that she belongs to us. I don't want them to see her. I don't want them looking at what's ours."

I was theirs? Interesting.

"Dominic," Alexander tried reasoning with him. "We need to do it by the book. You know what they said. It has to be done properly."

"You and your motherfucking rules," Dominic hissed, gripping me tighter than before. "We don't need them to make this work. You know we don't."

"Stop it!" Kairos thundered and jumped up to his feet, towering over us. "We spoke about this. You know what needs to be done. They need to see her. We have to get their approval, or—"

"Or what?" Dominic asked, turning me in his lap now. "They're going to kill us? Destroy—"

"Not us, you stupid idiot!" He came to us and pulled me out of Dominic's grip, and up to my legs. "Her! They're going to kill her!"

"Well, they can fucking try," Dominic argued and stood up seconds after me. "They're not taking her." He grabbed my hand, trying to pull me away from Kairos, but Kairos wasn't having it.

"Dom, you can either get in line or get the fuck out, but we are doing this properly. The Society knows why they're doing things this way. I don't want this to bite us on our asses, when we've worked so hard to repay the debt owed to them."

My eyes volleyed back and forth between them. If this continued, they wouldn't need me to fuck shit up. They would be their own downfall, and my job wouldn't be done.

But you promised, Echo. You promised you would take care of this as well.

I did fucking promise, but this incessant feeling in my heart wouldn't go away, even though I knew that these three wouldn't be suitable for the life they wanted to have.

Three little princes, fallen from their graces, trying to play the game of big boys and miserably failing. I was the perfect person for this job, but I didn't think it would be this hard to get on with it.

Pretending was the easy part, but actually standing here and getting my heart aligned with my brain was what had me fucked up and torn over what I needed to do.

I ripped my hand away from their grips and stepped aside, trying to think without their voices messing with my mind. I looked to my left, ignoring what was going on in front of me. My eyes zeroed in on a sign I had seen before.

It almost looked like a pentagram, etched into a headboard of the bed, but where the pentagram had five points, this one had six, with one pointing toward the top and the one toward the bottom with two on each side.

"What is that?" I pointed at the symbol, stopping their fucking bickering. My feet led me toward the bed, my hand already stretching to touch it, to feel it beneath my hand. "I've seen this sign before," I murmured, before turning toward them. "What does it mean?"

They kept quiet, uncomfortable even, but I would get my answers tonight.

"My father had this symbol in his study," I bit out. "What. Does. It. Mean?"

"It's an Aquarian Star." Alexander spoke first, earning glares from Dominic and Kairos. "What? She has the right to know."

"Not yet," Kairos hissed. "She still hasn't been approved."

"Oh, fuck off, Kai," Alexander said and came closer to me. "It›s a unicursal hexagram, representing great power."

I gawked at him, still not understanding what it was doing here. "I might be an orphan, Alexander, but I still know a hexagram when I see one. I didn't ask what it was in math, I'm asking what it's doing here?"

"It's a symbol of The Society," Kairos finally said. "A secret society not many are a part of. An underground Mafia if you wish, existing in the darkest parts of the world. We are a part of it."

"That's impossible." I chuckled. "My father was a good man. A great—"

"Your father was a monster," Dominic said without looking at me. "Just like mine is, just like Kairos's father is as well as Alexander's. They're all monsters pretending to be good people."

"You're lying," I hissed. "My dad was the best dad a girl could ever have."

"You should be thankful that's the memory you have of him."

"What is that supposed to mean?" I glanced at him.

"I know who you are, Echo. I know who your family was. What I don't know is how it's possible that they never found you in the system. I know they've looked," Dominic answered as he strolled toward me. "What I don't know is why you're carrying that knife with you."

"I-I—"

"Tell me, Echo. Did you know who invited you tonight?" Dominic asked, pushing the hair away from my face. "Did you know it would be the three of us here?"

He saw more than he should have. He saw what I didn't want him to see, and this was a problem.

"I don't know what you're talking about." I took a step back, hitting the nightstand with the back of my thighs. "I got an invitation to come here tonight. I can show it to you."

"I know you did because we sent it to you, but that wasn't my question." He smirked as he took off his suit jacket, dropping it onto the bed. "Who was the man you met early this morning?"

Motherfucking son of a bitch.

I thought I could play this game a little longer before revealing all my cards. My employer thought it would be a good thing to take out the three men whose families were responsible for the demise of my own—a poetic justice.

It would seem that the time of pretenses was coming to an end. If only I could shake off the feeling that there was more to all of this than anyone told me.

It wasn't as if I didn't know that my father wasn't a saint. It wasn't as if I didn't know that my own mother was a raging bitch, fucking whoever she could, because what waited for her at home wasn't satisfying enough, driving my father insane.

I just didn't know what the symbol meant, but now I knew.

I could feel the innocence I'd tried to portray slipping away from me. As I looked at the floor, I knew it was futile pretending anymore. If Dominic could figure out that not everything added up, the others could too.

"You got me, Dom." I chuckled and looked up at him. "Awww, don't pout, darling. It doesn't look very good on you." Tapping his cheek, I moved toward the middle of the room, feeling all of their eyes on me.

I sat down on the sofa chair in the corner and crossed my legs, pulling out the Swiss pocketknife I carried with me.

"This isn't going exactly according to my plan, but it's okay." I huffed. "I can adjust myself to the new circumstances."

"Adjust what?" Kairos asked, turning his body toward me, as if he could protect the other two from me. "Talk, dammit!"

"Tsk, Kairos. You are exactly as they said you would be. It truly is a shame that you were the man on the rooftop. I honestly wanted it to be somebody else, but I guess then none of us would get what they truly want tonight."

"Echo," Dominic all but growled and stepped between Alexander and Kairos. "What are you hiding from us?"

"Oh, plenty." I smiled. "I must say, seeing you tonight, Dominic, really threw me off my game. For a moment there, I forgot why I came." I opened the Swiss pocketknife, pulling out the blade hiding inside. "I didn't expect you here. These two…" I pointed at Kairos and Alexander. "I knew they would be here. In all honesty, only one of you is why I came tonight, and it isn't you, Dom." I glanced at Alexander. "Or you Alex."

Slowly, I stood up and walked toward Kairos and pressed the knife against his throat. "I came for you, darling." I snickered. "You know, my last night in Ignis, my official rebirth. The last night where I would carry this fucking last name that didn't belong to me."

"So you are Echo Selke, aren't you?" Dominic asked.

"Guilty." I shrugged. "I think it sounds much better than Echo Winslow."

Kairos gulped in front of me, his Adam's apple pressing against the blade. "So, you came to kill me?"

"I mean, killing you is a bit farfetched, don't you think?" I stood up and walked toward the door, feeling their eyes on my back. "But I must say," I grinned as I turned around to look at them, "it does give me an idea."

"Why do you think that we wouldn't kill you first?" Dominic asked, his eye twitching, his hands shaking. I reveled in the fact that I managed to throw them off. "Who was the man you met this morning, Echo?"

"None of your business," I sang. "But," I started, taking a deep breath. "You might want to reconsider trying to kill me tonight."

"We never wanted to kill you," Kairos grunted. "We wanted to keep you."

"Oh, yeah." I started laughing. "The Infernal Triumvirat, isn't that the name? The three boys make a pact with the Devil, and all they have to do is find the Maiden to keep them all together. Newsflash guys—that won't be me."

"You still won't be able to kill all three of us," Alexander spoke. "There's no way."

"You underestimate my power, babe. What was it that you called me? A sparrow?" I stepped toward him, but it was another body that slammed into me, blocking him from me that had me narrowing my eyes.

Dominic towered over me, breathing heavily. I knew that if he could, he would snap my neck within seconds. But he needed answers. He wanted to know who was after them.

"Who sent you?" he asked through gritted teeth.

"A fairy godmother?" I giggled. "Elves? Sir—"

"Stop playing around!" he roared and wrapped his hand around my throat, cutting off my oxygen intake. My back hit the wall as he pushed me away from Alexander and Kairos, the vein at his temple throbbing. "Who sent you?"

I smirked, looking in his eyes. With a hoarse throat, I said, "The Devil himself."

chapter ten

ECHO

I LOVED THEIR CONFUSED AND ANGRY FACES.

All the emotions running rampant, so strong they could be seen in the stiff posture of their bodies. They wore their hearts on their sleeves and I could only imagine all the thoughts going through their minds right now.

They didn't expect this.

They didn't expect me.

None of them ever expected that a poor orphan girl, suffocating in her own grief and sorrow, could be their downfall. The ones before them and the ones after them, they all made the same mistake—they underestimated me.

They thought that just because I wore a dress and a wobbly smile, I would be easy prey for their filthy games and their wicked dreams. They didn't know that the divine violence lived in individuals such as myself, patiently waiting in shadows for the day when justice would prevail. When the powers in hand would need to surrender.

The Society was yet another stain on our world that needed to be gone. Now that I knew their name and their M.O., I could share it with my sisters in The Order of Themis.

I'd been living in hell ever since my brother died, but two years ago, my misery became a burden heavier than I could carry. I just wanted it to stop. I wanted to stop feeling, stop remembering, thinking about everything that was taken away from me.

I almost succeeded.

I'd chased down a bottle of Adderall with vodka, hoping that the light shining through my windows would be the last one I would ever see. Deep inside my bones, I was done with the life that felt as if it was constantly trying to destroy me, to show me I didn't belong. I wanted to make it easier for everyone.

Easier for me.

And that's where they found me, gasping for breath, going in and out of consciousness, praying that the spasm in my body would soon stop. Praying that the void would finally swallow me whole, leaving behind nothing but a pile of bones no one really cared about.

But The Order of Themis cared.

Athanasya Erikhante cared, and they gave me a choice. They told me who killed my parents, who condemned me and my brother to darkness, all because they couldn't see eye to eye. She asked me then if I were truly ready to die, leaving nothing behind me.

No legacy.

No family.

"Do you really want to fall into oblivion, darling?" Athanasya asked. *"Or do you want them to pay for what happened to your family?"*

Guess what I chose?

If anger and the need for revenge were what fueled me in order to live, to survive, I couldn't complain. At least there was something holding me to this mortal realm. Something that helped me get up in the morning. Something that made all of this easier to bear and knowing that at the end of the road, those responsible for so much misery and pain would be destroyed.

These three miserable fucks were just a means to an end.

If only you truly believed in that, the inner bitch I often ignored piped in. They remind you of you. Deep inside, you know they could be yours forever if you allowed yourself to believe in it.

But I didn't.

Fairytale endings were nothing more but stories for little kids, too naïve and too young to know otherwise. I saw what promises of forever did to people. It changed them, took away who they truly were. I saw it happen to my mother, until the only thing she was filled with wasn't love but resentment toward my father, my brother and me.

I saw what it did to my father, knowing that his wife sought comfort in the arms of another. I felt it on my own skin when the pillars of our ivory tower shattered, falling down in pieces, and I could do nothing to stop it.

So, no. I didn't believe in forever, and least of all with these three.

The women who came before me were never found. Young girls filled with a need to be loved, to be cherished even if it was for one more night, lost their life to these three monsters because they didn't like who those girls were deep beneath the layers they showed the world.

They didn't like the reality of them and those poor women paid the price.

Insanity was a living, breathing thing in these three. No matter how much they wanted to believe that what they were doing was right, it was so fucking wrong. If they couldn't see it, then they shouldn't be a part of this world.

Dominic's hands went slack around my throat, his thumb softly pressed against my pulse point. I hated the shivering that racked my body from the way he pressed himself to me. I hated that they affected me at all.

"So what's it gonna be, Dom?" I licked my lips as the question softly rolled off my tongue. "Are you going to kill me now?"

"Shut up," he gritted out. "Shut up! Shut up! Shut up!" he screamed, shaking me against the wall. My back hit the hard surface behind me, but I kept my head away from it as much as possible.

A concussion wasn't something I needed tonight, but the rest of my body could take the brunt of injuries.

"Dominic!" Kairos roared behind him, but Dominic was lost to us. His demons had a grip on him that none of us could physically see. But it was there in his eyes. The darkness pushed forward, erasing all the light and good things that made him.

"Stop it!" Alexander butted in and threw Dominic off me. His big body hit the floor with a thud, and he groaned at the impact. I didn't dare move from the spot where Dominic had me pinned mere seconds ago.

I rubbed at the sore spot on my neck, working my throat through the burn that had me wincing as I tried to swallow.

Alexander moved the hair behind my ear, enveloping my face with his hands. "Are you okay?" he asked, almost whispering. The torment and that soft fucking touch almost unraveled me on the spot.

But I couldn't waver. Not now.

Pushing his hands off me, I moved away from him, going closer to the door. "I don't need you to save me, Alexander," I bit out. "Did you already forget what I just told you guys?"

"I didn't forget it," he gritted out. "I'm just choosing to ignore it. Contrary to popular belief, we aren't monsters."

"Really?" I huffed. "Then what do you call what just happened? Or, jeez, I don't know." I chuckled. "The bodies of all those girls that came here before me, only to end up dead."

"That's different," Kairos stepped in.

"How's it different, Kai?" I asked him, slowly inching closer and closer to the door. I pointed at Dominic. "He admitted that he killed one of them. So please, do tell me, which part of this story makes you three saints?"

"We did it for a reason, dammit!" Kairos thundered. "There's a reason for all of this."

"Is that what you tell yourself at night when the nightmares are stronger than the sweet dreams? Is that what I'm supposed to believe? That the three of you are some sort of saviors?" I laughed. "I didn't come here tonight to be just another number, you idiot. I came here for a reason."

In a split second, Kairos was in front of me. "You don't want to mess with us, Echo. Pretty little things like you shouldn't mess with big, bad wolves."

"Oh, darling," I murmured, lifting my hand toward his face. A five-o'clock shadow covered his jaw, and my fingers tingled as I brushed through them. "Your wickedness never scared me. I knew what I was getting into when I agreed to come here tonight." I looked at Alexander and then at Dominic who was still sitting on the floor, fuming.

I lifted myself on my tiptoes, reaching his ear. "But mine," I breathed out, "should terrify you."

His entire body stiffened, and I knew that if we were in any other situations, if he wasn't so distracted by everything that was happening, he would've seen me gripping my Swiss pocketknife. He would've noticed that a lamb wasn't a lamb at all, but a wicked wolf.

He would've noticed me lifting it as I whispered those soft words.

My hands were steady as I gripped the back of his neck with my left hand, playing with the strands of his hair. His chest was close to me, almost plastered to my own, and I knew I couldn't finish it all here.

I needed reinforcements. I had to alert Athanasya that it was time.

Moving back, I looked up, right into his eyes.

"I would say I'm sorry, but I'm not."

The first time I used a gun on somebody else, my body fought against me, and I retched, crying. Not because I cared for the life I'd taken, but because it freed me in ways that nothing else could.

Not even dancing.

The first time I used a knife to penetrate someone's skin, the flesh tearing apart made a squelching sound as the blood rushed out. It happened in a matter of seconds, but it felt as if hours passed before my knife retreated.

As I stood here, looking at him, I anticipated the same sound to reverberate in my ears.

"What are—" Kairos said, but he never managed to finish the sentence.

My hand flew forward, toward his thigh, and with swift moves, I strained my muscles as I stabbed him in his upper thigh.

"What the fuck!" he yelled out, stumbling backward with my Swiss pocketknife protruding from his leg. Alexander and Dominic jumped toward him, pulling him toward the bed, and I knew it was now or never.

"Try to catch me if you can." I laughed as I opened the door and bolted down the hallway.

The game had officially begun.

chapter eleven

ALEXANDER

"I'M GOING TO FUCKING KILL HER," KAIROS SEETHED as he limped through the hallway, all the way toward the exit. "Wring her neck, fuck her up, whatever is needed."

"Calm down," I murmured, hating that this night turned into this.

Dominic had yet to say another word, but I could feel his anger almost as if it were mine. He was always the one with volatile moods, but tonight I feared what would happen once he finally got his hands on Echo.

Especially after she wounded Kairos who was now walking around like a rabid wolf.

He pushed open the side door and slowly went down the stairs, leading toward the clearing right before the maze. It looked as if Halloween puked all over the place, with all the hanging decorations pointing at the entrance with one simple neon blinking arrow and enter if you dare right below it.

"I don't think this is such a good idea," I said, but neither one of them listened as they marched toward the entrance. The guards surrounded us from all sides but I knew that Kairos wanted to deal with this by himself.

"Kai—"

He stopped abruptly and turned toward me. "What, Alex?" he all but barked. "You don't want us to harm her? Too late for that."

"We don't even know what's happening?" I argued.

"Oh we know." He chuckled. "This has The Order of Themis written all over it. I'm just pissed off that I haven't seen it in any of the reports that were sent to me about Echo."

"But maybe—"

"Oh, give it a rest, Alex." Dominic spoke for the first time. "She isn't who we wanted her to be."

"And maybe that's the problem," I countered. "Maybe that was the problem with all of them. They're not supposed to be molded to us. We're all supposed to fit, no matter what."

"Well, this one will fit nicely at the bottom of the sea," Kairos said. "Once I'm done with her, she's going to wish she was never born."

"You don't mean that."

"Trust me, I do. She has no idea what she did, who she fucked with, but she will learn. Her death will be painful. I don't give a flying fuck what the Triumvirat says about unnecessary torture. This one deserves everything we throw at her."

"I just think—"

"Stop trying to save her, you fucking dumbass," Dominic bit out. "She. Isn't. Worth. It."

"I still think you're wrong." They completely ignored me, walking toward the maze. "How do we even know she went here?"

"Cameras, Alex. Security footage caught her entering it."

"Maybe she ran off of the island?" But even as I said that, I knew that wouldn't be true. The way she behaved with us, the way she stabbed Kairos, her hatred toward us, this wasn't a girl that would back down. "What if this is an ambush?"

"Look." Dominic stopped just before the entrance to the maze. "If you don't want to come with us, fine. We're going to do this on our own." I knew what he was saying. I understood the meaning behind those words even though he didn't say it out loud.

It was them or her. He wanted me to choose. If I stayed out of it, I could lose my best friends, the only two people who knew who I really was.

"Fine," I gritted out. "But we will hear her out first."

Dominic's pulled his lips into a smile filled with anything but happiness. "Whatever, Alex. You and I both know how this is going to end, and it won't be pretty."

"Dominic!" I yelled out as he ran toward the entrance, disappearing into the darkness of the maze, looking for our Maiden.

Or well, the girl that was supposed to be our Maiden. I doubted that any of them would ever try to do this again, but they had nothing to lose. Dominic was already on the road to hell, Kairos detached himself from us, and that left only me, standing on the side, observing, as if these two idiots didn't know how much I needed this.

This notion of family, of belonging.

But Dominic was right. I couldn't just stand on the side and do nothing. I couldn't watch them destroy everything we worked for, no matter how angry they were.

Everyone had a reason for the way they were, and there was more to Echo's story than she was telling us. There was more to all our stories, but those secrets were better left buried deep beneath. I just hoped they would never see the light of day.

Eerie music enveloped me into its dark embrace as soon as I stepped into the maze, with Dominic and Kairos nowhere in sight.

"Guys!" I yelled out, the sound of my voice echoing around us.

"Move your fucking ass, Alex." Dominic's voice came somewhere from the front, and I hurried to catch up with them.

I could barely see my own feet here, not to mention anything else, but as I came closer to them, I could see the two silhouettes walking in front of me.

"I thought you illuminated this fucking place, Kai," Dominic complained.

"I did."

"Then unless I'm losing my sight, I would like to know where the fuck are all those lights."

"My guess is as good as yours, Dom," Kairos said. "But if I really had to guess, I think that our little Maiden had something to do with it."

The only light cascading down on us through the leaves of the maze that covered the top part was the moonlight, but it wasn't enough.

"I don't like this," I said. "I don't like this at all."

"Why?" Dominic asked as he turned toward me. "Afraid of a little dark?"

"No, you ass. I don't like it because we can't see shit in front of us. I don't know if you remember, but she pretty much threatened to kill us back in the house."

Dominic opened his mouth to say something, but Kairos interrupted him.

"She won't do shit. This is a game for her, and just like us, she wants to play it until the very end."

"Then why do I feel like we're being—" I never managed to finish my sentence. The music suddenly cut off, the silence descending on us, feeding into paranoia, rocking through my body. I came closer to the two of them, trying to figure out where we were.

"Good evening, ladies and gentlemen," a melodic feminine voice cut through the air, making the hair at the nape of my neck stand up straight. "I hope everyone is having an amazing night. I'm sure that it will become even better."

"What the fuck is she doing?" Kairos hissed, moving forward as if he truly knew where he was going.

"There was this song, my mother used to sing to me when I was a little kid." She laughed into the mic. We hurried after Kairos who moved faster than I would've thought possible with his wound.

She missed all the important parts in his leg, but I knew him. It hurt like hell, yet he would never show it to us.

"I want you all to sing it out loud with me!"

And that's when we heard it. The crowd gathered outside of the maze, murmuring. The silence hugging us was louder than any song she could sing.

"Twinkle, twinkle little star," she started, and everyone joined her. "How I wonder what you are." They were like a choir, all singing along with her.

"Up above the world so high." I could hear the smile in her face. "How I wonder…" she trailed off, lowering her voice to a wicked whisper. "If you'll die."

"Fuck this shit," Dominic cursed and disappeared around the corner.

"Dammit." I ran after him. "Dom!"

"This is the way!" he shouted. "Just trust me."

The crowd quieted down as she said that last part. I wasn't sure if it was shock or just the amazement at what came out of her mouth.

"Oh, come on now. Don't go quiet on me. It is Samhain after all. Halloween, the most sacred night of all. And I am here to tell you all the secrets your seemingly perfect hosts have been hiding."

"Damn her," Kairos cursed.

"Secrets?" I asked. "Which secrets?"

But I knew which secrets. We all did. We all dreaded the day they would come out.

"Our favorite golden boy, Kairos. Those dark eyes, that dark hair, he could charm even the Devil himself and get away with it. But beneath all that charm, that perfect posture and a thousand-dollar suit, hides a little boy whose father never really loved him."

"That motherfucking b—" Kairos started cursing, but I was lost on every word she'd been saying.

"Daddy issues are apparently extremely common for guys as well, and here I thought girls were the only fucked-up people on the planet." The crowd laughed with her, their whispers and murmurs surrounding us from all sides.

The maze wasn't big enough to truly get lost, and with a crowd this size, we could almost hear what they were saying.

"But then little Kairos decided to leave home, after his daddy dearest fucked the only woman he ever truly loved—his sister."

"What?" Dominic and I asked at the same time, looking at Kairos.

He was frozen in place, his fists clenching and unclenching.

"I often wondered if his love for his sister went deeper than the simple sibling love. Was he actually really, really in love with her? After all, an apple doesn't fall far from the tree."

"Kairos," I said slowly, approaching him as a wounded animal. "Ignore her. Ignore everything she's saying."

"Step away from me, Alex," he grunted.

"I'm sorry. I didn't—"

"Whatever you're about to say, keep it to yourself," he said, looking at me. "I don't want your pity. Dakota... she... fuck!"

"We should do this more often." Echo chuckled through the speakers. "I think we could call it Halloween Central, where everyone's dirty laundry gets aired for all of you to hear. I mean, we all deserve honesty, right?"

"Yes!" The crowd agreed with her, and I knew they were enjoying this a lot more than she did.

"Anyway, moving on to our second contestant, Alexander Hale."

Gritting my teeth, I continued walking, hoping she would be somewhere in the maze. She had to stop. She had to stop all of this.

"Such a strong name, right? Such a strong man with a hero complex. But he couldn't save his own mother, how could he save anybody else?"

"She didn't," Dominic mumbled.

"Born in the Eastern World, Alexander Hale was seventh in line for the crown. I mean, I knew monarchs were weird and kinky, but I didn't know they had so many mental issues. Trust me, I'm not Miss Sunshine myself, but drowning my own kid, that's too harsh, even for me."

"What is she talking about, Alex?" Kairos asked from somewhere behind me, but I had only one goal in my mind.

To reach her and shut her up.

"Alex!" Dominic shouted after me.

"Not now, Dom. Not now."

"You see," Echo continued. "The funny thing about grief is that it can hit you out of nowhere, and it hit his mother too. Killing her daughter left an impact, but you know how it goes in royal families—mental illness is not something they wish to discuss. So one beautiful, summer night, she decided that living in the world without her daughter was too much to bear. And poor little, Alex," she mumbled.

"He found her there, on the perfect, porcelain floor in their bathroom, while crimson colored the tiles. He tried to stop it. Tried to gather her blood, thinking he could give it back to her. But her veins were wide open, her eyes lifeless, and the little boy wept for the mother he never truly knew. Because how could he? Love was not something easily shared in the royal families. Ever since then, he vowed he would find it one day."

"I'm going to rip her limbs, one by one," I bit out. "Cut her open."

"Alex!"

"Don't try to stop me, Kai. I thought she could be different. I thought that it was just a misunderstanding, but I can see her for what she is now. A wicked witch sent to destroy us all."

I looked up toward the top of the maze, recognizing the flowers growing there.

"We're close to the exit."

"I saved the best for the last," Echo piped in again, laughing at her own joke. "Dominic Talon."

All three of us stopped.

We knew it was coming. It was obvious that she wanted to humiliate us all, but Dominic's story was not something you could joke about. His was the story of betrayal, of the pain so severe that he never truly recovered.

"We all love our mothers. Right?" Echo asked the crowd, and they answered, "Yes!"

"And they love us as well. But Dominic's, well…" she trailed off.

"She loved him a little too much."

I looked at Dominic, at his rigid shoulders and the slow rising of his chest. All three of us had our demons to battle, but Dominic's lived inside of him, taking up permanent residence, and he didn't know how to get rid of them.

He tried, but nothing ever worked, and she was going to tell them all what it was that Dominic hid.

"Once upon a time, there was a seemingly perfect family. Yes, you got it right. Their last name was Talon. They hung out with this other seemingly perfect family, their kids playing together, but both families hid terrible secrets. You see, the father of the Talon family fucked the mother of this other family, while Mommy Talon found her escape in the much smaller body—in her son."

Gasps could be heard from around us, but none of it mattered.

Dominic was back in that time, back in her arms, and I knew that this would make a bigger impact than anything else did this entire night.

"He fought her at first, ran, tried asking his father for help, but his daddy told him that this was what boys were supposed to do. Even to this day, he can feel her hands on him, caressing him, wrapping around his dick, but he knows now she will never be able to touch him again."

"Dom," I approached him. "Dom, come back to us."

"You see, she would never be able to touch him again because this little boy made sure of it. Dominic Talon killed his own mother, in the middle of the bed she always kept him in."

Dominic's lower lip trembled. His entire body shook. I wanted to kill her for what she did to us tonight.

Here, I thought we were saving her from her miserable life, but she was playing us. All this time, the entire night, from the very moment when I introduced myself to her, she was playing a game.

Her voice was grating on my ears, the innocence she portrayed earlier now just another stain she managed to make. I hated that I almost fell for her lies and the fact that she felt like ours. She felt like mine. But I couldn't allow myself such thoughts.

She didn't belong to us. She never would, never could. Not after this.

The only place she belonged now was hell, and I was ready to send her there myself.

"Welcome to Tartarus, my boys." She cackled before the same music came back on.

Four could play this game, but she wouldn't be the winner. I would make sure of it.

chapter twelve

ECHO

THIS DAY WAS WHAT THE ORDER OF THEMIS TRAINED me for. This was what I was born for, yet I couldn't shake off this feeling of loss as if something was taken from me. Something extremely important.

I knew what needed to be done. I knew it ever since one of our messengers came to me with the task, after I alerted them of the package I'd received. But knowing it and doing it were two different things, and I hated myself for everything I said over the mic.

I wanted them broken. We wanted them broken, terrified, lost, just how most of us were lost, but I never thought that saving all those vile things aloud would remind me that this wasn't what I signed up for. Did I want them to pay for all their sins? Yes, yes I did.

But was this the right way?

My heart broke as I went through those vile things The Order gave me to read. Everything would've been fine if I hadn't had to read the ones for Dominic. Maybe he was a monster, they all were, but killing them would've been easier than destroying their public image in front of all their friends.

As soon as I ran out of that room, I alerted Athanasya that the plan was in motion, that we needed to act now, or they would've had to pull me off the island. She was ready, just how she always was, but I had no idea that the plan would involve gathering all heir peers around the maze while I spewed all those vicious and dark things they kept hidden from the rest of the world.

I wanted justice, not to humiliate them.

Themis, the Greek Goddess of justice our Order got the name from, often wore a blindfold on pictures and statues that represented her. I wondered now how many times she judged wrongly just because she didn't see the entire picture?

Was I just like her now, judging these three men when I didn't have the entire picture in front of me?

But they were vicious. They were cruel. They would've killed you just like all those other girls.

Would they? I wasn't so sure about it anymore, especially not after the way that Alexander cared for me, or the way that Kairos carried me. Even in his madness, Dominic seemed to want me more than he wanted me gone. Did I screw this up?

"They're almost out of the maze." Athanasya spoke from behind me, and as I turned around, I could see her in her white toga, standing at the entrance to the old church that was here long before the Adair family bought this island. "You know what you need to do."

Her blond hair swayed in the wind, and she looked more than ever like a true Goddess, judging others without proof.

"Are you sure we're doing the right thing?" I dared to ask. Even though I hated the way her eyes blazed toward me and her lips set into a thin line, I had to know.

Were we truly the heroes or were we the villains in this story?

"Echo Selene Selke," she spoke as she glided toward me. "Are you questioning our methods?"

"No." I shook my head. "I'm questioning the things we think we know and all the other facts we don't. Sometimes it's very easy to mistake good from evil, and what might seem like doing the right thing, might be the complete opposite one."

"We are doing the right thing," she answered. "You are doing the right thing by ridding this world of these men. Just remember all the girls who disappeared from here. How did their families feel? Their friends? Do you think that these men cared if they were doing the wrong thing? They just took and took and took until there was nothing else to take. They discarded them, just like that, without thinking about the consequences. You know it as much as I do. I don't understand why you're wavering right now."

Taking a deep breath, I turned toward the maze, waiting for them to emerge. "I just," I started. "It feels wrong, doing this to them. I don't know why."

I could feel her eyes on me, calculating, observing. I hated that she could see how uncertain I was of this whole thing.

I hated even more that those words so callously uttered by me were what made me stop and think about this whole thing. I hated injustice. I hated the people that sat on their golden thrones, having everything they ever wanted, while others had nothing.

I hated the division between people. I hated even more the fact that those three men were connected to the families that ended up destroying mine.

I knew that Dominic's father and my mother chose each other instead of their spouses. I knew that the Adair family ordered a hit on my father, and my mother was just collateral damage in the conflict. But reading all those other things and knowing that they weren't having such perfect lives as they made other people think, made me rethink if they were the true villains of this story or if it was me.

But they killed all those girls. They made them disappear.

Did they? Were they the culprits or was it someone else?

"Remember your duty, Echo," Athanasya reminded me. "Remember who you are and why you are here. Don't let your heart lead this game. Use your brain."

I turned around to argue with her, but she was already gone, and I knew what that meant. I knew it with every fiber of my body because I could feel their gazes on my back.

Like the three devils, Kairos, Alexander, and Dominic emerged from the maze. Kairos was limping, and I couldn't stop myself from smirking at his obvious distress.

Judging from the looks on their faces as they strolled over the clearing, they weren't coming here to make me their Maiden. They were coming to kill me.

They would first need to catch me.

I ran inside the church, almost choking at the pungent, moldy smell that belonged to the place. But it was perfect for what was coming next. As the doors slammed behind me, I ran all the way to the altar, my heart hammering in my chest, slamming against my ribs. The only other time the adrenaline coursed through me like this was when I danced.

Floating.

Weightless.

I hoped I could have my fun before the inevitable came.

The Order had many rules, some of which I hated, others I admired, but the one rule they didn't give a fuck about was how we decided to finish our tasks. Before this night was over, I wanted all three of them on their knees, begging me to spare them all this pain and misery I was going to bring.

But we were going to play first.

I unzipped the dress I was wearing, letting it fall to the floor as I slowed down in front of the altar. My black, lacy underwear was hidden underneath the black pair of shorts, and as I stepped out of the pile made out of my dress, I walked toward the bench where Athanasya left my crop top.

Pulling it on, I took my spot right next to the broken statue of Jesus and dropped the knives my mentor had left me for later on.

People always had a choice, and these three would be given one—surrender or die.

The wind whistled through the cracks of the old church, and I wondered why it was made in the first place. The first pilgrims often made their churches on the land, avoiding islands like the plague because it was too difficult to transfer the necessary equipment.

Yet this one was made, and the nerdy part of me wanted to explore and see why.

Maybe some other time.

The doors slammed open, the wind rushing in and hitting me as the three of them entered this place.

Even Alexander, kind and soft Alexander, looked like he wanted to murder me on the spot. I knew the feeling, knew it all too well actually, but I wasn't the reason why they were meeting their doom.

They were.

Their choices were what led them to me. The things they did were what put the target on their backs and why The Order wanted them gone. But even more than that, their connection with The

Society would be their ultimate downfall.

"Are you just going to keep standing there, looking at me, or are you going to do something?" I asked when none of them moved from the entrance.

I was poking the bear, but I loved playing around with things I shouldn't. And these three, they were the forbidden fruit that I couldn't resist.

"Are you going to stand there the whole night, or are you going to come down to actually talk to us?" Kairos asked, crossing his arms across his chest.

A small smirk played on his face, but there was nothing playful in the energy they were all sending my way. They wanted blood, and they would get it. I wasn't strong enough to take all three of them, but I was strong enough to distract them long enough.

I took the first step down the stairs, smiling the whole time. "Maybe we should meet halfway?" I said. "Or maybe you guys are afraid of what I might be keeping underneath this uniform?"

I didn't miss the way their eyes drank me in. They no doubt wanted me dead, but they also wanted to devour me—that much was obvious. And I would be lying to myself if I said that I didn't want them too.

I wanted them to shatter my world, to take everything, before I sent them into the void.

"You guys have two choices—surrender and tell me everything you know about The Society..." Dominic started laughing at this. "Or die." I shrugged.

"Really?" It was Alexander who stepped forward, surpassing Kairos. "You really think that you can take all three of us?"

"I mean, I could try. Which is why I don't understand why all three of you are standing so far away as if I could hurt you all at the same time."

"You already did enough," Kairos bit out. "You did more than you should've, and for that, our darling little sparrow, you will pay."

I thought they were stalling at first, but as I kept looking at Kairos, I missed seeing Dominic rushing toward me from the side.

He must have moved before I could see it, and the crazed expression he wore was enough to chill the blood in my veins. But I wouldn't go down without a fight. I needed to give The Order enough time to bring in the police.

Evidence was hidden all over the Manor, and it was just a matter of time before the authorities came in.

I ducked down as Dominic went straight for my head, barely avoiding his fists. They were stronger, but I was faster.

He swiveled around and went down on me, but I managed to roll away. In the moment where it felt as if time was suspended, I could see the young boy who always made me feel pretty, reflecting in his eyes.

I hurt him, and no matter what, I never wanted to fuck him up in such a way.

Unfortunately, I couldn't dwell on what I should and shouldn't have done. With one quick kick of my leg to his side, he grunted, stumbling to his left.

Another pair of hands landed on my shoulders and as I looked up, I could see Alexander holding me to the ground.

Kairos came in front of me and kneeled between my legs, spreading them wide.

"Hello, little Sparrow," he murmured as he dove toward my neck, biting at my flesh. "You taste so heavenly, but we all know that there's poison rushing through these veins."

My breathing was labored, the need to run, to hide, riding me hard, but I couldn't move.

"Screw you, Kairos!"

"Gladly, darling."

He gripped the elastic band of my running shorts and tore them apart, throwing the ruined fabric to the side. Alexander gripped my chin and pulled my head up, his fingers digging into my skin as if he could make me disappear this way.

"Pretty little Sparrow," Alexander murmured, his lips just a breath away from mine. "You've been a very bad girl." His teeth clamped down on my bottom lip. Instead of screaming or trying to move away, the moan erupted from my chest when his tongue came out, soothing the place he just bit.

"You liked that, didn›t you?" Alexander chuckled as another pair of hands landed on my bare thighs, kneading the heated flesh. "You like us dominating you."

"N-No." I shook my head, but we all knew I was lying. "Let me go," I hissed.

"Never," Kairos growled. "You brought this on yourself. Now you'll pay."

"No, no, no." But they didn't listen, and neither did my traitorous body.

Kairos pulled my hips closer to him, kissing, licking, biting at the sensitive flesh. As if that weren't enough to push me over the edge, Dominic joined in, flicking my nipples beneath my crop top, pulling and squeezing, while Alexander devoured my mouth as if it belonged to him.

"You're ours now, Sparrow," Alexander murmured against my lips. "Whether you like it or not, you're ours and you've been a very bad girl."

"I-I don't want this," I whimpered when Kairos's lips closed around my clit. "Please!"

"Your mouth is saying one thing," Kairos said, his voice vibrating against my opening. "But your body can't lie. You want us. You want this."

"No!"

"Submit to us," Dominic growled from above, squeezing my boob to the point of pain. "And maybe we could forgive your little outburst earlier. Submit, Echo!"

"Never!"

Kairos chuckled. "As you wish."

His tongue was relentless, his fingers masterfully playing me like a guitar, knowing exactly where to press and where to squeeze. As he entered me, my back arched off the floor, and I wanted to jump out of my skin.

Alexander kissed my cheek before he stood up, unbuttoning his slacks and letting them fall on the ground. Dominic did the same, completely removing his clothes. I hated seeing the scars on his stomach as he finally removed his shirt.

Alexander kneeled again, and without thinking, my hand wrapped around his hard dick, going up and down.

"Such a good girl, Echo," Alexander murmured, praising me, and something inside of me snapped.

It was too much—they were too much. I could feel it rushing through my veins, all the way to the pit of my stomach and down through my folds, where Kairos relentlessly stroked, bit and caressed my skin as if the anger still didn't shine in his eyes.

Alexander pressed his dick to my mouth and like a good girl, I opened, swallowing his head.

"Yes," he hissed, working his hips, and pushing his dick deeper into my mouth. Dominic wrapped his hand around my throat, pressing his thumb against my pulse point, and as he increased the pressure, I exploded.

My body shook, my hands on Dominic, on Alexander, but neither one of them stopped what they were doing. My movements were uncoordinated, my body not my own, and I needed more.

So much more.

I could hear another zipper opening and the soft thump as the clothes fell, but I couldn't move my head. I couldn't see what was happening while Dominic held me in his chokehold.

"Such a pretty pussy," Kairos purred, kissing the top of my thigh. "Such a wicked, little girl," he murmured, pressing the crown of his dick to my opening. "You belong to us, Echo. You will always belong to us."

I wanted to deny it. I wanted to stay and run at the same time, but they had me where they wanted me, and like a slave to my own desires, I let them. I let them do whatever the fuck they wanted to.

Kairos nudged his dick through my opening, and my body spasmed again, knowing what was about to come. He pressed one hand against my pelvis and in one sharp stroke, he entered me, filling me up to the brim.

I moaned against Alexander's dick, squeezing Dominic tighter, all four of us groaning and moaning at the same time. Alexander increased his rhythm, Dominic fucked my hand, and Kairos slammed into me like a man possessed. As if he needed more, just like I did.

"Are you going to come for us, pretty girl?" Kairos asked just as Alexander moved away from me. "Are you going to explode around my cock like a good girl?"

"Y-Yes," I moaned, throwing my head backward.

Dominic stepped aside just as Kairos lifted me up. I wrapped my legs around his waist as he stood up with me in his arms and with his dick inside of me.

He pressed me against the altar, right next to the broken statue of Jesus. I would have laughed if I wasn't overwhelmed with sensations.

My pussy squeezed his hard dick, needing him to move.

"Please," I moaned as he laid me down on the flat surface. "Kairos!"

"Is this what you need?" he asked as he swiveled his hips, hitting that sweet, sweet spot inside of me.

"Yes!"

"No, you don't get to have it nice and easy tonight," he growled against my lips and pulled his dick almost all the way out, before slamming into me again. "You've been a very bad girl, Echo." He bit down on my collarbone, marking me. "And you know what bad girls get?"

"Please," I begged. "I'll be a good girl."

"Running away from us," he grunted, slamming into me like a man possessed. "Revealing all of our darkest secrets." Oh God. My pussy was spasming around him, my body readying itself for another avalanche. "Are you going to do that again?"

"No! Please."

His fingers thrummed against my clit, bringing me closer and closer and closer—

"Fuck!" I screamed out. As I looked at the side, I saw Alexander and Dominic with their eyes on us, stroking each other.

My body betrayed me, vibrating, shaking as Kairos savagely chased his own release, murmuring sweet words into my ear, praising me, telling me how much he wanted to spank me for everything I had done. How much he wanted to kill me, but he couldn't.

A lone tear escaped from my eye because I knew. I knew that this was the end. I knew they would truly hate me after the next part, and I wanted to hate myself as well.

Alexander and Dominic groaned, kissing each other as their cum covered their bodies—Dominic's naked torso and Alexander's clothes.

Kairos threw his head backward, the veins at his neck protruding as he screamed out my name, spilling inside of me.

I had to get away from him. I had to get away from all three of them.

But I couldn't do that with him holding me so tightly as if he never wanted to let me go. My eyes zeroed in on one of the knives I'd left on the ground, I begged, prayed even, that I wouldn't have to use it tonight.

Kairos caressed my hair as he lifted me up and started carrying me around the room. He put me down on one of the benches and unbuttoned his shirt. Tears cascaded down my face, my heart breaking for something I would never have.

Maybe it was the aftershocks from sex that had me emotional, but if the circumstances were different, I would've allowed them to take me with them. If I were somebody else and if they weren't monsters I was sent to apprehend, I would've allowed myself to open my heart for them.

Kairos draped his shirt around my shoulders, and only then did I realize that he somehow removed my crop top without me noticing. I looked up at him, at that vein throbbing at his temple, and I knew he was still angry with me.

But he cared enough to have me covered. Even the other two, Alexander and Dominic, seemed to have calmed down a bit.

I couldn't look at them. Couldn't let them see my tears, so I did what I always did best. I got up and went closer to the altar, wiping my tears with the sleeves of Kairos's shirt. This next part would hurt like a bitch, but I had to do it.

I had to do it for my brother and all those other kids, men and women who got fucked over in life.

I kneeled and took the knife into my hand.

"We need to talk, Echo," Kairos said. "What just happened—"

"Means nothing," I said as I turned around, plastering a smile on my face. "Did you think that just because you fucked me senseless I would suddenly forget who you are?"

"You don't have all the facts," Alexander butted in. "What they've been telling you—"

The doors of the church opened and Athanasya walked in with other members in tow.

"What we've been telling her and sharing with her is the truth. You three don't deserve to have this life." Athanasya smiled at me. "Seize them."

The men from The Order rushed in, and before any of them could react, they had Dominic and Alexander on their knees, holding their hands behind them, with guns pointed at their temples. Kairos looked at them, then at me. As the first police officer walked into the church, he lunged.

"You motherfucking—"

But he never got to go too far.

I stumbled backward as he hit into me, but my body wasn't what stopped his advances. He took a step backward, stumbling on his legs, and that's when I saw it.

The knife I was holding lodged deep in his chest.

"No," I breathed out, my eyes flickering from the knife to his eyes.

Blood trickled down his chest just as he fell to his knees.

I was immovable. Powerless.

"I guess you got what you came here for, Sparrow," he rasped, blood slowly rushing through his mouth. "You managed to kill me."

"No!" Dominic wailed, fighting against the guards. "Kairos!"

"Atta girl!" Athanasya laughed as I watched him fall in front of my eyes. "That's how it's done!" she cheered on.

"What did you do, Echo?" Alexander cried out, and it was enough to sober me up.

"I did what I needed to do, darling." I smiled and walked over to him. "You look perfect on your knees," I murmured and kissed his cheek. "But I would like to hear you beg, Alex. Beg me to save your friend."

"Never," he spat out. "When we get our hands on you, you will be the one begging."

I bopped his nose and stood up. "I'm counting on it, pretty boy."

The rest of the police officers rushed in, already going for the two standing members of the Triumvirat. They already had all the details, all the evidence needed to put them away for a very long time.

And if my heart broke a bit as Dominic kept crying out for Kairos, I would never admit it.

This was, after all, just business.

Athanasya hugged me as soon as I came over to her. "You did well. Better than well. We were all outside as you finished your little, well, you know." She chuckled. "I didn't know you were such a good actress," she continued, walking me out of the church.

I wasn't a good actress—not at all.

epilogue

ECHO

Ten years later

SEAGULLS CAWED ABOVE THE SEA STRETCHING IN front of my house, creating a perfect melody for the hot summer day at the coast of Cresthill. Oftentimes people asked why I chose to build one of my houses here, but it was simple really—lack of people.

And two weeks during the summer was the only time I was allowed to run away from a stuffy and suffocating Arkenheim where Selke Incorporate was based. No matter how much I loved my job, my people, my company, I needed this time to recharge and regroup.

Ten years ago, from this exact date, I vowed to myself that I would find time to enjoy little things, and if sipping coffee while watching the sunset was one of them, so be it.

The cliffs beneath the house that hid the beach were what attracted me to this place. A population of less than fifty thousand was what cemented my decision to buy it. My little paradise, far away from everything and everyone I knew.

I chose to ignore the pit that opened in my stomach as soon as I opened my eyes this morning. It'd been ten years but every Samhain, I felt again like that young girl. And every single Samhain, I had the same dream—Kairos's face as he tumbled down. Dominic's screams and Alexander's hatred.

I promised myself I would put that behind—put them behind—and enjoy my life as much as I could. And grief—it came and went. These two days were always harder to get through, but I'd learned to cope. I managed my moods better than I did years ago, and I had a family now.

My grandma might have passed away five years after I finally came home, but The Order of Themis was my family in every sense of that word. Athanasya still pestered me constantly, and we all tried to get together at least once a year, considering that most of us had other jobs.

Like taking care of family legacy. Making sure that the thousands of employees of Selke Inc. still had a job which gave them a roof over their head. It didn't really matter that the happiness I was constantly chasing never truly came to me.

I was safe. I was loved and no one could ever take it back from me.

Leander, a man I'd met three years ago, showed me that love didn't have to be toxic. It didn't have to hurt in order to feel something. And if he bored me to death some of the nights with his missionary pose and dull conversations that weren't really satisfying, I could overlook those.

He made me happy—or well—as happy as I could be.

A doorbell rang, echoing through the house, breaking through my peaceful afternoon.

It couldn't be Leander, he had a key, and he was supposed to come later in the evening. I chose to spend these two days completely alone, to grieve and be sad on my own terms, without anybody else telling me that things would get better.

But other than him, I didn't expect anyone else.

I lowered the cup of coffee I was holding in my hand and placed it on the table, then slowly walked toward the dresser in my room. Old habits die hard, and it wasn't like the underworld never saw my face.

Opening the third drawer, I pulled out the small, throwing knife and hid it on the inside of my sleeve. Next, I walked toward the control room and checked to see who was standing in front of the gate.

"The mailman?" I frowned. I didn't order anything.

I buzzed him in, curious to see what he had for me, and slowly walked downstairs toward the main door, waiting for him to arrive.

Gravel scrunched underneath the tires of his van. As soon as I heard the doors opening and closing, I opened the front door, deciding to wait for him at the entrance.

"Good afternoon," he said first, pulling a big, black box from the passenger seat. "I was worried that no one was home."

"Morning," I mumbled, while my fingers partially stayed on the handle of the knife. "Sorry, I was out on the terrace."

He smiled, walking toward me. "That's okay." Within seconds, he was in front of me, lowering the box to the ground and pulling out a letter from his pocket. "Ms..." he narrowed his eyes on the scribbled writing on the letter. "Echo Selke?" He looked at me.

"That would be me."

"I just need you to sign something for me." He ran toward the van, pulled out a small device from the passenger seat, and walked back toward me. "You have a really nice place here."

"Thank you." I grinned. As he turned the device toward me, indicating to sign here and there, I pushed the knife into the waistband of my leggings when he wasn't looking.

"Well." He bent down, placed the black envelope on top of the box and picked it up before turning toward me. "This one is for you."

I took the box with both hands, surprised by how heavy it was. "Whoa. Are there stones inside?" I laughed.

"I have no idea, ma'am, but it was sent as a priority."

"Priority?" I frowned.

"Yep." He nodded. "I better get going. Have a nice day and thank you for opening that gate."

"Yeah," I murmured, looking at the box. "You too."

I didn't wait for him to leave before going back inside the house and locking the door behind me. Memory after a memory slammed into me as I stared at the handwriting on top of the envelope. Golden ink, black envelope, and a black box.

"You've gotta be kidding me."

I placed the box on top of the small table in the foyer and stared at it.

"It couldn't be."

Pulling out a knife, I ripped through the black tape that was holding the box together and slowly opened the lid.

"Holy shit!" I jumped away from the wretched object when I saw what was hiding inside.

A whole fucking hand, with a ring I knew all too well, sat at the bottom of the box, surrounded by torn black lace.

"No, no, no." I shook my head, staring at the goddamn contents as if they would somehow give me answers I needed. I bought him that fucking ring for our anniversary, and while he annoyed the fuck out of me most of the time, I didn't want him dead.

I didn't want him to get his hand severed.

I picked up the letter next, almost knowing what would be inside. It's been ten fucking years, but those men could hold a grudge like no other. Kairos died that night, but the other two—the other two swore they would destroy me.

Did they get out? And if they did, when? Why didn't I know about it?

My hands were steady as I tore through the envelope, finding a white piece of paper inside. My gut churned as I let the envelope fall to the floor, opening the letter addressed to me.

We know all your secrets, our little sparrow. But this time, we will be playing our game. And this time, you won't be able to get away. We've been waiting for ten years for this moment to come. Get ready because we are coming for you.

The Infernal Triumvirat.

Those motherfucking shit ass fucks!

I crumpled the paper and threw it against the wall, shaking from rage.

Ten years. Ten fucking years of peace and they were coming to destroy it. But if they thought I would wait like a good little girl, they had another think coming. Because that girl they knew back then was gone.

There was only one thing I could do, and I believed that they were coming. And even though their message seemed as if they just wanted me for themselves—I knew better.

They were coming to kill me, but they wouldn't make it so easy. They would torture me, get back at me for everything they went through.

I ran upstairs, back to my room, and picked up my mobile phone, dialing the one person who was always there for me.

One ring…two…three…"Come on," I mumbled, then she answered. "Echo?"

"Houston, we have a big fucking problem."

to be continued

The story of Echo and the guys continues in
Funeral for Dreams, coming out in 2023.

also by l.k. reid

THE RAPTURE SERIES
RICOCHET
EQUILIBRIUM
OBLIVION

SECRETS OF WINWORTH
APATHY
TEMPTATION

STANDALONES
HOW OUR HEARTS BREAK
SERENDIPITY (A NOVELLA)

ANTHOLOGIES
ONCE UPON A NIGHTMARE

acknowledgments

It truly does take an entire village to write and publish a book, and I wouldn't be able to do this without all the amazing people I have in my life.

We all know I am not the most organized person when it comes to the other side of publishing, and if it wasn't for my PA Julia Murray, I probably would be a bigger mess than I am now. Thank you for setting me straight.

I would probably have stopped writing and publishing a long time ago if it wasn't for my amazing author friends (you know who you are). Thank you for always being there for me.

To Zoe, Zozo, I cannot even tell you how much I appreciate having you in my life.

To Amy, Brianna, Kendra, Emily, Mandy, and Jessa—words cannot express how thankful I am for your help.

And to Mary, my amazing editor who still didn't disown me (I don't know how or why). It is extremely hard to find someone you can really trust with your work, knowing that they will do their best. This is the eighth book/story for me and I am glad I have Mary to help me out with my words.

To you, readers. I wouldn't be here if it wasn't for you.

And last, but not least—music. For always being here for me.

about the author

L.K. Reid is a dark romance author who hates slow walkers and people being mean for no reason. She lives with her two cats, Freya and Athena, and she's still figuring out the whole "adult" thingy.

In her opinion, Halloween should be a public holiday. She also has a small obsession with all things historical—especially Greek mythology. During high school, she wanted to be an archaeologist, and ended up studying law, but obviously neither one of those professions worked out.

If she isn't writing, she's most probably watching horror movies, listening to music, reading, or plotting upcoming books.

Stay in touch

.instagram.com/authorlkreid

pinterest.com/authorlkreid

facebook.com/authorlkreid

.goodreads.com/authorlkreid

The Reid Cult